E.G. FOLEY

A GRYPHON CHRONICLES CHRISTMAS NOVELLA

JAKE & THE
GINGERBREAD WARS

Books by E.G. Foley

The Complete Gryphon Chronicles Series:
The Lost Heir (The Gryphon Chronicles, Book One)
Jake & The Giant (The Gryphon Chronicles, Book Two)
The Dark Portal (The Gryphon Chronicles, Book Three)
Jake & The Gingerbread Wars (A Gryphon Chronicles Christmas)
Rise of Allies (The Gryphon Chronicles, Book Four)
Secrets of the Deep (The Gryphon Chronicles, Book Five)
The Black Fortress (The Gryphon Chronicles, Book Six)

50 States of Fear Series:
The Haunted Plantation (50 States of Fear: Alabama)
Bringing Home Bigfoot (50 States of Fear: Arkansas)
Leader of the Pack (50 States of Fear: Colorado)
The Dork and the Deathray (50 States of Fear: Alaska)

Credits & Copyright

I heard the bells on Christmas Day
Their old, familiar carols play
And wild and sweet
The words repeat
Of peace on earth, goodwill to men.

~Henry Wadsworth Longfellow

TABLE OF CONTENTS

CHAPTER ONE
A Very Merry Mishap

"I know the Christmas pageant in the village means a lot to Aunt Ramona. I just don't see why I should have to be in it," Jake grumbled, only half in jest, as they wandered out of yet another shop. "Honestly—did you see the fake beard I have to wear?"

His three companions laughed, for they had.

It was dreadful.

"But you have to be our St. Joseph, Jake. You're the tallest," said Isabelle.

Jake looked askance at her.

Of course, his golden-haired cousin was quite content with her (very fitting) pageant role as the angel who would go and call the shepherds.

"Ah, well." He let out a longsuffering sigh, but deep down, he supposed he didn't *really* mind being made a fool of for his elderly aunt's sake at Christmas. It was just that, as a tough ex-street kid, he had a certain reputation to keep up. Especially now that it turned out he was an earl. "All I know is I'm going to feel completely stupid in that getup, standing out there in front. Everybody staring at me. Why can't I just hide in the back with Archie as one of the Three Wise Men?"

"You? A wise man? Sorry, Jake, you're not that good an actor," Dani O'Dell (their pageant Mary) teased. "I know!" The freckled redhead turned to him with a mischievous grin. "You could be the donkey!"

"Ha, *ha*." Though he gave her a sardonic look, even Jake could not help laughing any more than he could hide the holiday twinkle in his eyes.

It was all a little bewildering, in truth. He had never felt this ridiculously happy two days before Christmas.

For the first time ever, the holidays had put a kind of spell on him beyond anything that even a good witch as powerful as Aunt Ramona could've conjured. There was magic in the air.

Christmas magic.

He could feel it in the afternoon's light snowfall wafting over London. It dusted the cobbled streets around them like sugar and trimmed the bonnets and top hats of passing ladies and gents with its delicate, frozen lace.

This year he thought it very beautiful, but last year at this time he would have hated it, mainly because he would've been sleeping out in the cold most nights. Last year, instead of smiling at his fellow man with general goodwill, he would have been eyeing up the passersby with the goal of picking their pockets, watching for packages and coin purses he could steal.

Everything was different now, including Christmas.

The odd, merry mood had taken hold of him a few days ago, stamping his face with a slightly dazed smile, as if he had eaten a whole roly-poly pudding by himself. He felt so strange.

In the past, all the Christmases he could remember had been ordeals of torture, more or less. It was a day that made most of the kids back at the orphanage wish they were dead.

Ah, but this year, for the first time, Jake had something of a family. Not parents, they were dead, but two cousins and a few random adults who did not bother him too badly. (Very well, he quite adored them—not that he would ever admit to any such mushy sentiments out loud.)

He also had Dani O'Dell, his little Irish sidekick from the rookery. The carrot-head had taken charge of their Christmas shopping excursion, as she was wont to do in most matters.

"Indefatigable," Archie remarked, sauntering along, hands in pockets, as he watched the redhead march ahead of them, her mittened hands balled up at her sides.

Jake nodded vaguely, though he only understood about half the words that ever came out of the boy genius's mouth.

Dani stopped at the corner and glanced around, choosing which row of shops they'd tackle next. "Hurry up, you lot!" She beckoned to them when there was a break in the steady flow of carriages and stagecoaches, hansom cabs and delivery wagons rumbling by in both directions.

All the world was hurrying to finish up their yuletide preparations.

As for Jake and the others, their mission this day was almost complete.

Possibly the best thing about his new life as the rightful Earl of Griffon was that he now had the means to make Christmas a little less miserable for the orphans and assorted street urchins he had left behind in his old life.

If Father Christmas or St. Nick or Santa Claus or whatever the useless lout wanted to call himself could not be bothered to visit the orphans—which he never did—well then, Jake had decided, he would jolly well do it himself.

At all the different toymakers and linen drapers and food stalls they had visited today on their quest to gather presents, they had ordered everything sent to Beacon House, awaiting Christmas Eve delivery.

The trick was how to make the gifts appear magically, so the orphans would think that Santa had done it. They were still working on that. Maybe one of Great-Great Aunt Ramona's magic spells would do the trick...

Jake wished he could see their faces when they woke up on Christmas morning to find that Santa had finally remembered them, especially the little ones, like Petey, a six-year-old who used to follow him around everywhere and tried to be just like him. *Poor kid.*

"Isabelle." When they joined Dani on the corner, she gave the older girl a probing stare. "How are you holding up? Do you need a break?"

"Hullo? What about us?" Jake asked, nodding at Archie.

The other boy nodded eagerly. "We could use a break, too. Christmas shopping is *exhausting.*"

"We're hungry," Jake agreed.

Dani looked at him. "What a shock."

Isabelle laughed. "I'm doing fine, thanks. Better than expected, actually."

They all knew that being in the crowded city was difficult on Isabelle as an empath, picking up on the emotions of everyone around her.

She shrugged, reading the doubt on their faces—or, more likely, sensing it in their hearts. "Maybe I'm getting stronger or finally learning how to shield myself. But I think somehow it's just easier to be out and about this time of year." She glanced around at the busy street. "Most people just seem to be in a...kinder mood."

The four of them exchanged wry, knowing smiles, then paused to appreciate the holiday spirit that warmed the frosty air.

Carolers nearby sang "God Rest Ye, Merry Gentlemen." All the wrought-iron lampposts wore garlands of evergreen boughs tied with red ribbons. Sleigh bells jangled on the harnesses of the carriage horses trotting past.

But as to the question of whether to take a break from shopping, the mouth-watering smell of sweet cinnamon somethings baking somewhere nearby decided the matter for them.

"Maybe a snack *is* in order." Isabelle inhaled the enticing odor with a dreamy smile. "Is that gingerbread?"

Jake flashed a grin. "Let's go find out!"

They ran. Well, the boys did.

Isabelle was much too well bred to go pounding down an elegant London street like a wild heathen, thanks to strict training from her governess, Miss Helena.

Dani managed (just barely) to restrain herself to a sedate walk alongside the older girl, determined to be as ladylike as the older girl someday.

In any case, the boys were the first to reach what turned out to be not one, but two pastry shops crammed into one tall, narrow brick building.

On the left, a few steps led upward into a glittering, pastel jewel box of a bakery, whose sign read in flowing calligraphy: *Chez Marie Pâtisserie Parissiene.*

On the right, a few steps led downward into a snug, rustic, cozy space rather like a hunting lodge, its doorway proudly hung with the Union Jack and announcing in plain block letters: *Bob's British Bakery.*

The boys had difficulty choosing which way to go first.

If they had waited for Isabelle, the empath soon could have told them that the two renowned pastry chefs—Marie and Bob—had once been partners, but now were sworn foes. They did everything in their power to antagonize each other.

4   E.G. FOLEY

Especially Bob, who had got his heart broken.

But, being boys, Jake and Archie were oblivious to romantic matters for the most part. They went whooping down the stairs, past the pinecone garland and the life-sized toy soldier just inside the door.

"Welcome, gents," the mustachioed owner drawled. Bob himself was leaning idly against the counter talking about the latest sporting news with a few of his male customers: the London prizefights and the winter foxhunts going on out in the countryside.

The boys nodded back to him, then suddenly stopped in their tracks. "Ho! Look at that!"

They immediately rushed over to gawk at the gingerbread display: a towering castle with candy banners flying from the turrets. All around it, little gingerbread knights and soldiers were arranged as though tending to their duties.

There were even gingerbread horses with white-frosted manes, and gingerbread cannons loaded with peppermint cannonballs.

Meanwhile, the girls had been unable to resist the glowing chandeliers and silk-hung walls of the French-style pâtisserie upstairs. As they entered, Isabelle told Dani that "pâtisserie" was simply the French word for a pastry shop; Dani thought it a fun word to say and kept repeating it.

As it turned out, the owner, Mademoiselle Marie, had no intention of being outdone by her ex-beau, Bob, during this most important shopping season. She *also* had made a dazzling gingerbread display to lure in customers. But—she being French—hers was of course the height of elegance and whimsy, and in every way superior. One only had to ask her to confirm that this was so.

Marie had made a gingerbread Versailles with candy swans in the fountain and meringue shepherdesses tending marshmallow sheep. Wee cookie courtiers in service to the Sun King strolled through the candy formal gardens; gentlemanly ginger-men, fashionably frosted; noble cavaliers, prepared to fight for the honor of their crispy kingdom.

While the boys bought chocolate-dipped pretzel lances below, the girls gazed in rapturous wonder at Marie's marvel of baking artistry.

"What a lot of frou-frou," Archie said, glancing around, brow furrowed, when the boys joined them upstairs a few minutes later.

"Yes...isn't it wonderful?" Isabelle said breathlessly.

"Where have you two been?" Dani asked.

The boys told them about Bob's British Bakery downstairs, and the girls hurried down to the lower level to explore it, too.

The boys followed, and while Jake went to show the girls the castle, Archie was drawn to an old photograph on the wall of a cavalry regiment. Apparently Bob used to be a soldier.

"Looks like they're having a contest of some kind." Jake nodded at the sign beside the gingerbread castle inviting customers to vote on which display they thought was better.

"Aha, clever way of getting more shoppers in the door," Archie said as he rejoined them.

"I don't think that's entirely the reason these two have made a contest of it," Isabelle said under her breath.

They all glanced curiously at her, but she was too discreet to gossip about the ongoing lovers' quarrel she sensed between the two bakers.

Jake shrugged off her mysterious remark with a decisive nod. "We should vote, too."

"Let's!" Dani said. "I need to look at both of them again."

Bob glanced over in amusement as the kids barreled back up the stairs into Marie's dainty boutique to consider their choices.

Having already determined he liked the castle better, for it reminded him of the one he had inherited from his father, Jake wandered off hungrily to look around Marie's fanciful shop and choose another snack.

He had never tried French pastries before, but looking around, it was impossible not to be impressed. He had to admit those French knew their food, despite the centuries-old love-hate relationship between England and France. Thankfully, there had not been bloodshed for many years between the two countries, but most good loyal Englishmen, like most French folk, could give you a list off the top of their heads why their country was better than the one across the channel. And yet, at the same time, they secretly admired certain traits about each other.

Clothes, for example.

Every London lady simply had to fill her wardrobe with fine French gowns, while men's English tailoring ruled the streets of Paris.

As for food, well, most of the world had long since concluded that the French beat everyone in that category, except for maybe the

Italians. Ah, but the British were better at sports and bred better horses, and, at least in their own opinion, told funnier jokes.

It was true the French were traditionally better at dealing out a witty insult with devastating style. But when it came down to a fight, Jake thought, ha! His country was better at war, as evidenced by the fact that they had trounced the French in the last one.

Ah, but of course all that was long before he was born, those bloody days of Napoleon versus England's Iron Duke. And as an avid fan of all things edible, Jake was quite prepared to let bygones be bygones. He drifted through the cramped, crowded aisles of Marie's shop, marveling at the exotic French sweets on offer.

He read the dainty placards with all the unfamiliar foreign names. The pastries were all such exquisite little artworks it almost seemed a shame to eat them.

There were rows of *Mont Blancs*, small whipped cream mountains with a candy perched atop each crest. There were *Opéras* with many thin layers of sponge cake held together by coffee syrup and topped with shiny chocolate ganache.

There was *Strawberry Savarin* dusted with powdered sugar and *Tarte Tatin*, a glossy puff pastry cradling caramelized apples. There were individual lemon soufflés and something called *Canelé*: tiny golden-brown bundt cakes. There were *éclairs* and *Napoleons*, *Fondant au Chocolat* and *Forêt Noire*. There were macaroons and *Lunette aux Abricots*, danishes that looked like pastry blankets wrapped around sleeping golden apricot babies.

But what stood out in glory, second only to the gingerbread Versailles, were the magnificent edible "Christmas trees" capping the ends of each aisle.

Jake heard a lady explaining to her husband that these were called *Croquembouche*, though she had never seen them made so large before. Creampuffs had been stacked up into pyramids like edible pine trees, held together by long ribbons of caramel.

His mouth watering at the splendid sight, Jake was wondering if his stomach had enough capacity for him to eat one all by himself. Probably yes, he mused, when suddenly, he noticed a whiz of motion from the corner of his eye.

The barest hint of a sparkle-trail followed as something went speeding along the top shelves of the shop, flush against the walls.

Startled, he looked twice, turning to catch a better glimpse, but he was too slow. It was already gone, the red-and-green sparkle-trail fading so fast that he wondered if he had imagined it.

Intrigued, he took a few steps out of the aisle and scanned the upper shelves, brow furrowed. Whatever it was, it had disappeared, but he was sure he had seen something.

Indeed, now that he noticed it, he could feel the slight tingling sensation at his nape that usually alerted him when something supernatural was close by.

Obviously, his first thought was to wonder if the shop was haunted. To be sure, there were ghosts all over London. It wouldn't have surprised him.

But as far as he knew, only fairies left sparkle-trails. Not even their nearest cousins, the pixies, had that particular trait. He knew because he had just met some in Wales.

Hold on—! An astonishing question suddenly filled his mind. *Is that how she's doing this—baking such amazing things? Has this French pastry lady got fairies helping her?*

Unfair advantage! Jake huffed in surprise, instantly indignant on British Bob's behalf. Well, typical, he thought. Leave it to a Frenchwoman to make her own rules.

His instant suspicion of Mademoiselle Marie would have to be forgiven.

Though he was only twelve, all British males were warned from an early age to resist as best they could those magnificent, impossible French ladies, who were famous worldwide for doing whatever they pleased.

Humph. Nobody liked a cheater.

He shook his head in disapproval, determined to even the odds in British Bob's favor—and to learn the secret of Marie's exquisite skill. He started prowling around the small, crowded shop, on the hunt for the fairy or whatever it was that had made that sparkle-trail.

Small as fairies were—five inches tall or so—it could be hiding anywhere. Jake searched the high shelves, the back of his neck tingling away, but he never saw anything—and yet he got the feeling after a few minutes that the fairy had definitely noticed *him* hunting for it.

Aye, he could feel it watching him. The creature must've realized he was on to its trickery. *I am going to find you...*

He searched the shop for several minutes more while his

companions bought a few goodies to eat. Stalking down the middle aisle, he sensed that he was closing in. It was close, very close...

Determined to take it by surprise, he suddenly jumped out of the middle aisle and spun in midair like a startled cat, facing down the next aisle. "Ha!"

The other customers looked at him strangely.

Alas, the fairy was already gone.

Once again, he saw nothing but the green-and-red sparkles already fading. *No worries. You're a fast little devil, but you're mine.*

Hmm. As he continued his hunt, collecting a couple of treats to buy along the way, he mused on the fact that although he had met his share of fairies, he had never seen a sparkle-trail in those strong colors before.

The royal garden fairies he knew usually had gold or silver or pastel-colored sparkles.

Was there some specific kind of Christmas fairy? he wondered. Burning with curiosity, he crept down the aisle, and then stood on his toes to peer warily behind one shelf's display of cherry-laced *Clafoutis.*

The creature he was hunting must've started getting nervous about the danger of being caught, for suddenly, without Jake even noticing, it struck back.

Apparently, it hoped to get rid of him by causing a distraction.

"Timberrrr!" a small voice taunted.

And with that, the *Croquembouche* Christmas tree behind Jake started tipping over. He whirled around as the unseen speaker sped off with a snicker, red-and-green sparkles in its wake.

Jake gasped when he saw the *Croquembouche* toppling, sending a snowstorm of sugar-dusted cream puffs and macaroons flying through the air.

He started forward automatically, lifting his hands to use his telekinesis to try to save it—but thankfully, he stopped himself in time. It would have been a disaster for him to use his magical powers in public.

And so, there was nothing he could do but stand there and watch the beautiful, edible Christmas tree go crashing to the ground, destroyed.

It then occurred to him that, as the person standing closest to it, he was about to take the blame.

Aw, crud. Jake let out a sigh. *Story of my life.*

CHAPTER TWO
The Way the Cookie Crumbles

Jake hated being blamed for things he didn't do, but for some reason, that always happened to him.

Customers shouted and everyone leaped out of the way of the falling pastry tree. There were cries of dismay, then everybody in the shop turned in shock and glared at him.

He stepped back, wondering if there was any point in telling them it wasn't his fault. It was the fairy.

Right.

They'd haul him off to Bedlam.

A woman with dark eyes, a sharp nose, and a smudge of flour on her cheek came rushing out of the back with a look of horror on her face. "What have you done?" Her accent promptly informed him that this must be Marie, the *artiste* herself. "You will pay for zis!"

"Excuse me, it wasn't my fault," Jake said sternly.

He couldn't help it. Perhaps it was ungallant of him to refute her, but facts were facts. Besides, she was a cheater anyway, with her secret fairy helper. Unfair advantage over poor British Bob.

"*Mon Dieu!* Do you have any idea how many hours my staff and I have slaved over zat?"

"Aha, your staff, right," he drawled.

"What?" she spat. "Where is your mozeur?"

"My what?"

"Your mamma!"

He stiffened. "I don't think that's any of your business, madam."

"*Garçon horrible!* Not even an *apologie*? Give me back those boxes. You are not worzy to eat my creations!" She snatched the treats he'd chosen out of his hands.

"Ma'am, I did not knock over your...thing."

(He was not sure how to pronounce it.)

"Ha!" She snapped her floury fingers in his face. "Get out of my shop, and don't come back until you learn how to walk upright like a *personne*, not a shimpanzee!"

"Now, look here," he started in lordly high dudgeon. "I will pay for this mishap, even though it wasn't my fault." He took out his small coin purse with a look of reproach. "But I *don't* appreciate your calling me a liar."

Mademoiselle ignored him, suddenly glaring past Jake toward the doorway of her shop. *"You."*

Jake turned and saw British Bob leaning against the doorframe, looking amused by all the commotion.

"You put him up to zis!"

"My dear, I have no idea what you are talking about," Bob said with a mild smirk under his mustache.

"You sent this little *monstre* in here to wreck my shop!"

He folded his arms across his chest and said calmly, "Nonsense, you daft harpy. I told you the *Croquembouche* was a bridge too far, but no, you had to best me. Well, there you have it. Right again."

Marie unleashed a stream of angry French verbiage on him; Bob replied with maddeningly cool British sarcasm, and the two rival pastry chefs proceeded to spread the Christmas cheer by hollering at each other in the middle of the shop, ignoring all their customers— and unbeknownst to them, attracting the attention of a passing constable.

Jake's friends ran to him.

"What did you do now?" Dani exclaimed.

"Oh, thanks a lot," he retorted.

"I say! What is going on in here?" a deep voice boomed from the doorway behind British Bob.

Everyone looked over; Jake blanched. *Blimey.*

Of all the bobbies to respond, Jake saw it was none other than his old mustachioed nemesis from his pickpocket days, Constable Arthur Flanagan.

The policeman's stare homed right in on Jake; recognition flashed in his eyes, then he brushed his way past the angry bakers. "Well, well. I should've known I'd find this one smack in the midst of all the trouble."

"Good afternoon, Constable Flanagan," Jake said courteously through gritted teeth. Ah, the memories.

"Why, look at you, all dressed up like a gentl'man. Never thought I'd see the day!" Flanagan declared as he stepped in. "Got a whole new life these days, from what I read in the papers, don't ye? But I see you're still the same young rascal I remember. Up to your old tricks, eh, Jakey boy?"

"It wasn't me!"

The bobby laughed heartily. "Ah, how I've missed hearin' you say that." Then he quit laughing and resumed his usual warning glower. "What did you steal from this lady's shop?"

"Wot?" Jake cried, sounding like his old pickpocket self once more. "Nuffin'!"

"*Non,* Constable," Marie snapped. "He did not steal from my shop; he only half destroyed it."

"Tempest in a teapot as usual, constable," Bob said. "But that's the French for you, innit? Look, the lad already got out his coin to pay for the trouble—"

"He'd better pay," she retorted.

"Ah, leave him alone, Marie. He's just a kid and it's nearly Christmas," Bob grumbled. "I'm sure 'twas an accident."

"Fine. Just get him out of my shop. And don't come back!" she added, glaring at Jake.

"I said I was sorry!" Jake exclaimed, tossing the coin in her direction as Constable Flanagan took hold of his ear.

"Come on, you." He led him firmly out of the shop and deposited him in the snow outside.

"Ow!"

"You might be quite the fine young lord now, laddie, but I'm on to you," the bobby warned, wagging a finger in his face. "You'd better watch your step. The rest of the world might bow and scrape to ye now, but I don't care in the least if you're the Earl of Griffon or the Prince of Siam, mark me? You'll not be goin' about causin' trouble like you used to."

Dani elbowed Jake hard in the ribs to shut him up before he gave the tart rejoinder on the tip of his tongue.

"Happy Christmas, Constable Flanagan," she offered.

The bobby tipped his dark helmet to her. "Miss O'Dell. You look after 'im. He's not so grand nowadays that I won't still toss him in the

Clink if he earns it."

"I will, sir. Er, give our best to your family?"

"Move along, children. *His Lordship* has caused enough mischief for one day." The bobby waved them off, raising a bushy red eyebrow at Jake, who, scowling, righted his coat and harrumphed.

Dani took his left arm and Archie took his right, and they both steered him away from there before he was tempted to say something he'd regret.

Constable Flanagan kept an eye on them until they had gone off safely down the lane, then he moved along, on patrol once again.

"What just happened in there?" Archie demanded.

"I'll have you know, it wasn't me who knocked over that what-cha-call-it tree thing."

"Then who did?" Dani asked.

He pulled his arms indignantly out of their grasps. "A fairy or something," he muttered.

"What?" they exclaimed in unison.

"There's something weird going on in that shop—and I intend to get to the bottom of it," he declared. "How dare that woman yell at me like that? I do *not* deserve to be publicly humiliated for something I didn't even do!"

"A fairy," Archie repeated.

"Aye! That French lady's using magic as an unfair advantage over Bob, and that's not right! So, you know what I'm going to do?"

"Um, nothing?" Dani suggested.

Jake shook his head. "I'm coming back here tonight when the shop is closed, and I'm going to catch that meddling little creature and remove it. That'll teach Miss Hoity Toity Mademoiselle how we deal with cheaters here in England!"

"That's a terrible idea," Dani said. "She told you never to come back. If you get caught in her shop a second time, she could have you arrested."

"Especially after hours, when it's closed," Archie added.

"Well then. I won't get caught," he said.

"And why do you want to do this?" Isabelle asked.

"Obviously—it's a matter of honor!" Jake declared. "I am the Earl of Griffon and she called me a liar in front of all those people! Intolerable! Then Flanagan insulting me, too, when I didn't even do anything. I am not a pickpocket anymore! I never cause trouble!"

"Wellll," the others said in response.

Jake glowered. "Are you with me or not? Well, do as you like," he said, waving them off impatiently. "I can catch that rotten fairy by myself, if need be. But you're mad if you think I'm just goin' to take this. I will *not* be insulted and unjustly accused. A gentleman has to defend his honor. Right, Archie?"

"Uh, I guess so."

"Besides, Marie's a cheater, anyway. British Bob deserves a fair fight in that contest of theirs. A matter of honor, I say. My own—and England's!"

Isabelle shook her head with a sigh. "You're daft."

Jake ignored his oh-so-mature elder cousin, and held up his fist to rally his two most reliable followers, the younger pair. "For England!"

Well, it was worth a shot, anyway. But Archie and Dani merely exchanged a dubious glance.

CHAPTER THREE
'Twas the Night

J ake's run-in with the bobby had rather dashed their merry mood, so they returned to Everton House and cheered themselves up by devouring all the goodies they had managed to buy before getting thrown out of the dueling bakeries.

Unfortunately, too many sweets in too short a time had a predictable effect. All four grew slightly queasy, which resulted in them griping at each other.

This was most unlike them, but nobody felt well after practically pouring sugar down their gullets for an hour. They all felt rather stupid for having done this to themselves and started blaming each other: "Why did you make me eat that?"

Isabelle got a headache. Dani ran around in circles with her dog for half an hour, giggling in the most annoying fashion, before suddenly collapsing in exhaustion on the couch.

Archie shocked them all with an uncharacteristic outburst of fury over a smudge on his spectacles. "Blast it, I just cleaned these!"

He threw his glasses across the room, and they might have broken if Jake had not caught them from several feet away, using his telekinesis. He levitated them slowly back to his usually good-natured cousin.

Archie cleared his throat. "Sorry," he mumbled. "I don't know what came over me. I don't feel so well." Indeed, he looked a little green around the gills. Archie stiffly marched out of the parlor to go and clean his glasses again.

Jake sprawled back in his arm chair once more, holding his stomach. He felt as fat as Santa Claus.

He frowned at the empty bakery boxes, still littered with

powdered sugar like a sprinkling of snow. He usually had an iron stomach, but even he felt a little nauseated. "I hope there wasn't something wrong with those sweets."

"Of course not. We just ate too much of them. Ugh. We're a bunch of pigs." Dani pulled a pillow over her head with a groan.

They ate a very small supper of *salad* and *vegetables* that evening, and though they had pretty well digested their splurge of sweets, they were all still grumpy.

Jake figured the others were irked at themselves for wasting the afternoon trying to recover from the unpleasant aftereffects of their binge. But as for him, he knew exactly why he was still in a bad mood. Constable Flanagan, mainly.

And that arrogant French lady.

And, of course, the unseen fairy who had made a fool out of him in public. But no matter.

He'd soon have his revenge. He was already plotting the pest's removal from the bakery. He would need some assistance, however.

The question was, who would help him?

Isabelle still had no interest in the whole affair. Dani didn't dare participate, for fear of angering Aunt Ramona and losing her position as paid companion to the older girl. That left Archie, who had his doubts about Jake's mad scheme, but was too loyal to make him go it alone.

Jake feared he was a bad enough influence on his straight-arrow cousin. But he assured Archie that he wouldn't have to do any breaking and entering. He'd do that part himself.

The boy genius would be stationed outside the shop to keep watch and warn him if anyone was coming.

Like another policeman.

For his part, Jake had no qualms about sneaking into the bakery. He had certain dubious skills from his pickpocket days, like how to pick a lock. He also had a gift for stealth when the situation required.

Flanagan's warning to behave himself still rang in his ears, but it wasn't as though he'd be breaking into the shop to steal any more sweets. *Blech.* On the contrary, he'd be quite happy if he did not have to look at another cake or piece of candy until Easter.

Tonight's adventure would only be a pest-removal mission—but there was one problem. He had no idea how to catch a fairy.

For that reason, he called in the best expert he knew on all matters pertaining to the fey folk: Gladwin Lightwing of the Queen's own royal garden fairies.

Gladwin sometimes served as fairy courier to Queen Victoria herself. She had been very busy lately delivering Christmas greeting cards for the royal family. In any case, Jake sent her an Inkbug message, asking her to come to Everton House at her earliest convenience.

She arrived after supper, buzzing in through one of the unused chimneys upstairs. Their favorite fairy came flying down the grand staircase and into the parlor, where the four of them were still strewn about like so many sacks of potatoes.

Even the Gryphon was lazy, curled up in front of the fireplace, enjoying a snooze on that dark winter's evening. Red's golden beak rested on his front paws, his scarlet wings tucked against his tawny lion sides.

He looked up pleasantly when Gladwin came speeding in, leaving a golden sparkle-trail behind her.

The five-inch fairy was dressed in her tiny fur-trimmed coat for the season. It had holes in the back so her magnificent, sparkly wings could poke through.

"Good evening, everybody! Hullo, Jake. I got your Inkbug message. What's afoot?" She landed on the end table beside the sofa, the sparkles still fading behind her. Bracing her tiny hands on her waist, she looked around at all of them with a frown. "What's wrong with you all?"

"We're in a bad mood," Dani said.

Then Jake explained all that had happened that day, and what he meant to do about it.

Gladwin stared at him for a moment, her wingtips wiggling uncertainly as she pondered Jake's proposal of capturing the fairy in the bake shop. "And why do you want to do this, exactly?"

"Because he made a fool of me! And because he's helping Marie cheat in the baking contest against Bob."

"So? It's just a baking contest," Gladwin said with vexing logic.

"Would you just trust me?" Jake exclaimed. "I can't explain it. I just *know* there's something funny going on in that shop. I'll bet you bones to biscuits that this fairy is behind it!"

"Calm down," she chided. "Sweet bees' wings, you are all out of temper tonight. Humph! Well, I certainly don't see the need for violence, if you insist on taking this fey person into custody. You don't want to get any of the fairy nations angry at you, Jake. We might squabble and make war amongst ourselves from time to time, but let a human wrong a fairy, and all the fey folk tend to band together against your kind. Trust me, nobody wants that."

"Of course not, but I'm telling you, this is no ordinary fairy. He or she is a menace."

Gladwin furrowed her brow, then glanced over at Red. "What do you think?"

The Gryphon shrugged his scarlet wings.

Gladwin turned back to Jake with a thoughtful frown. "I'm sure it's all just a big misunderstanding. The fairy probably just got scared and felt he had to defend himself. But very well. If one of my people is in there causing trouble, then, as an emissary of the Queen, I suppose I should at least step in and try to have a word with him. Maybe we just need to hear his side of the story."

Jake was relieved that she had agreed to cooperate, but he still had his doubts. "Thanks, Gladwin. Knew I could count on you. All the same, I doubt this little fellow's going to come out of that shop peacefully. More likely, we're going to have to drag him out kicking and screaming. And there's the problem. He's too fast. We're going to need some way to stop him or at least slow him down long enough to make him talk to us."

She hesitated. "The fairy freeze spell would do it."

"Great! You can teach it to me," Jake said. "I'll go get my wand." He started to head for the hidden safe in the cellar, where Aunt Ramona insisted all magical equipment be stored away when not in use.

Wands were not toys, after all.

"Jake, come back!" Gladwin called. "You don't need your wand. I cannot teach you this spell."

"Why not?" He paused and turned around.

"It's forbidden for any of us to teach it to the non-fey." She squared her tiny shoulders. "If it comes down to it, I will use it on him myself so he can't get away."

At that moment, the grandfather clock beside the wall started bonging. Jake glanced at it. "Nine o'clock. I think that's when the shop closes. That means we can go. C'mon, Arch."

While the boys ran to get their coats, Red jumped to his feet and shook himself awake. He would provide their transportation—and keep a protective eye on them, too.

Before returning to the others, Jake snuck out to the stables that belonged to Everton House, the London mansion he had inherited from his parents, as opposed to Griffon Castle out in the country.

Inside the stable, Jake found an old gunnysack made of rough brown burlap. He shook the last few pieces of the horses' sweet grain out of it. Then he folded it up small, tucked it into his coat, and hurried back to the house.

He was willing to give Gladwin a chance to talk to the trickster in the bakery, but privately, Jake had no intention of going in there unprepared.

If she could not persuade the troublemaker to leave *Chez Marie* by his own free will, then Jake would follow his simpler plan of catch and release. Namely, he would catch the fairy in the gunnysack, then set him free somewhere out in the country beyond the boundaries of London, where he could not bother anyone.

Once Jake returned to the house and Archie said he was ready, the boys climbed on the Gryphon's back. They held on tight as Red pushed off from an upstairs balcony, lifting into the frigid night sky with his powerful wing beats.

Gladwin kept pace with them, flying alongside Jake's shoulder.

It was the first time Archie had seen London at night from the air. True, he was an inventor of flying machines and other strange contraptions, but, as reckless as he was in the pursuit of science, not even the boy genius was mad enough to attempt flying the Mighty Pigeon at night.

He ooh'ed and ahh'ed in wonder at the rows of streetlamps like tiny golden beads lining the grand thoroughfares, like Regent Street and Pall Mall.

Big Ben glowed in the dark, while Westminster Abbey and Buckingham Palace were adorned with green wreaths and scarlet ribbons for the holiday. White wisps of smoke rose from all the chimneys, and groups of carolers below went singing door to door, collecting coins for some charity.

The boys smiled at the sight of tiny-looking ice skaters swirling along the Serpentine lake in Hyde Park.

But as charming as London was at this time of year, Jake was all business; he pointed to show Red the way.

At last, the Gryphon swooped down from the starry sky, landing on the roof of the building across from the bakery. That way, the boys could survey the area before going in, make sure the coast was clear.

"That's the place?" Gladwin asked, fluttering in midair.

Jake nodded.

Archie scanned the dark street through the Vampire Monocle, one of his favorite devices they had unearthed on their last adventure. It provided the wearer with excellent night vision. "No sign of your friend, the bobby," he reported.

"Good. Take us down, Red."

The Gryphon waited for a carriage to pass below before plunging off the side of the roof and coasting down gracefully to the snowy street outside the double-bakery building. The boys got off the Gryphon's back.

"Good luck, Jake!" Archie whispered, backing into the shadows to keep watch through the Vampire Monocle.

"Remember, three raps on the window if you see anyone coming."

"Righty-ho." Archie leaned against the wall, becoming almost invisible in the shadows.

Gladwin murmured that she would go in first. Jake watched her fly up to the bakery's roof, then she disappeared, diving in through the chimney.

A few minutes later, he could see her sparkle-trail glowing through the shop's bay window. She buzzed around inside, making sure that Mademoiselle Marie and her employees were not still in there working.

By now, ten o'clock, the fabulous pâtisserie was empty. The bakers had baked, the cake decorators had decorated, the clerk had counted the day's money, and the cleaners had cleaned up.

All was quiet.

Jake waited with a tingle of nervous anticipation running across his skin. His heart pounded. Sneaking in after hours like this—why, it felt like old times. Good thing he had grown adept at sneaking around back in his thieving days. He steadied himself for the mission at hand when Gladwin appeared at the front door.

She unlocked it for him from the inside. It gave a low creak as Jake eased it open. Then he and Red slipped into the shop.

Time to hunt the fairy.

CHAPTER FOUR
A Bittersweet Feud

As soon as he stepped into the dark shop, Jake gagged a bit, nearly overcome by the sticky-sweet smell after having gorged himself on treats all day. He shook off the nausea with a will, turning as Gladwin flew nearer.

"You two look around out here," she whispered. "I'll go check the kitchen."

Jake nodded and she zoomed away, trailing golden sparkles down the center aisle and back behind the bakery counters.

"Careful, Red! Mind your wings," Jake scolded in a whisper as his big, lion-sized pet padded through the little, cluttered shop.

Jake shook his head and crept down the nearest aisle. He barely dared wonder who would take the blame this time if Red knocked over another of Marie's creations.

Putting the earlier mishap out of his mind, he concentrated on finding the fairy, or whatever sort of creature was lurking in this shop. Red also listened keenly, his small, tufted ears pricked up, his eagle eyes shining with a faint golden glow in the darkness.

Suddenly, Jake thought he heard the tiniest murmur of voices coming from somewhere near the end of the aisle.

He moved in silence, placing one foot carefully after the other, just like in his pickpocket days.

Yes, he definitely heard someone calling from just around the corner of the aisle. A very small voice, possibly that of a fairy. He couldn't be sure.

It sounded female. "Rollio, sweet Rollio! Wherefore art thou, Rollio?"

Jake furrowed his brow.

Holding his breath to avoid making even the slightest sound, he sidled up to the end of the aisle, where another *Croquembouche* stood proudly. (He moved extra careful around it.) Lowering himself to a crouched position beside it, he stole a stealthy glance around the corner of the aisle.

He kept his gaze up high, expecting to spot the mischievous fairy flying around in here somewhere. So the second little voice, and the flicker of motion down low on the floor, came as a surprise.

"Juniette! I am here!"

Jake lowered his gaze and looked straight at the speakers. He blinked rapidly, certain his eyes were playing tricks on him. But no.

The speakers were still there.

Down on the floor, mere inches high, two little gingerbread cookies ran to meet each other and shared a quick embrace.

"At last! Oh, Rollio!"

"My sweet Juniette!"

Jake's eyebrows slowly lifted. Red appeared by his side, stared at the gingerbread couple for a moment, and then turned to him, as if to say, *Explain.*

Jake shook his head in bewilderment and shrugged.

"Hurry, my sweet!" Rollio said. "We must away!"

Noting the gingerbread boy's smart icing helmet, Jake was sure he recognized British Bob's style of decorating his ginger-soldiers.

As for Juniette, her pink-frosting hair certainly marked her as one of Mademoiselle Marie's creations.

"Oh, how I've missed you!" the tiny girl cookie cried. "Together at last!"

"Come, my dainty crumb. We must not linger!" Rollio warned. "My brothers are climbing the battle ladders even now, and your father's troops won't be far off. We must hide before they find us!"

"If only our families did not forbid our love!" said Juniette.

"Hurry, take my hand."

A gingerbread person doesn't actually have a hand, per se, just a nice rounded arm. But that didn't stop the cookie couple. They held on to each other as best they could and raced away with tiny, tapping footsteps as they fled across the shop.

Jake could do nothing but stare in lingering astonishment as Rollio and Juniette disappeared in the direction of the kitchen.

He had barely just recovered his wits after this impossible sight when a horrible thought gripped him.

Great Scott! *The treats in this shop come to life?* He blanched and clutched his stomach, wondering if he had murdered sentient beings by eating all those goodies today.

"Becaw?"

Jake ignored the Gryphon for the moment and wildly searched the nearest shelves to see if any of the other edibles were coming to life. Thank goodness, he quickly concluded in relief that only the gingerbread display seemed to be affected. But how?

He needed a closer look. That fairy must have something to do with it, he thought. Fairy magic could be very mysterious.

Red followed as Jake tiptoed toward Marie's gingerbread Versailles. What he saw made him freeze with such astonishment that Red could have knocked him over with one of his feathers.

The gingerbread Versailles was in an uproar.

Preparations for a battle were underway—and just in time, too.

For, as Rollio had warned, British Bob's ginger-soldiers presently invaded somehow from downstairs.

Marie's ginger-courtiers received the first wave of the attack with typical French aplomb. The gingerbread folk rushed into battle, British Bob's little knights charging, Marie's frou-frou courtiers fencing with the gusto of the famous Musketeers to defend their homeland.

They launched a barrage of candy cannonballs from their cookie cannons. They dueled with swizzle sticks and hurled spurts of red icing at each other.

"How...can this...be happening?" Jake whispered in a daze.

Red shook his feathered head. "Caw..."

Jake glanced at the Gryphon. He had never seen the noble beast looking so confused before.

The only logical explanation he could think of was that the fairy he had detected here today had put some kind of magic spell on the gingerbread displays.

Maybe they only came to life at night, for Jake was certain the gingerbread folk had been motionless—normal, inanimate, baked goods—when they had visited earlier today.

All of a sudden, he and Red heard a frantic cry from the direction of the kitchen. "Help!"

Jake gasped, snapping back to awareness. "Gladwin!"

They ran, abandoning the mystery of the gingerbread war in progress, and rushed toward the kitchen.

As he ran to Gladwin's aid, Jake took care to watch where he was going. He wasn't sure where Rollio and Juniette were hiding, and he dreaded the thought of accidentally stepping on them.

He dodged around the shop counter and charged through the doorway into the bakery's kitchen.

It was darker in the back, with only one window over the sink, but the smells changed from the cloying sweetness of baked goods to a hint of cleaning fluids in the air. Marie's staff had left their work areas in ship-shape for the morning. But unfortunately, whatever sort of scuffle had gone on between Gladwin and the fairy hiding in the shop had caused a mess.

"Gladwin, where are you?" Jake whispered loudly, glancing around in the doorway, with Red right behind him.

He heard a little cough and splashing coming from a spot near the wall, and ran to where Gladwin was angrily pulling herself up out of a milk pail.

"Blimey. Are you all right?"

She sputtered, her wet wings sagging. "Yes, yes, I'm fine. Oh, that ungrateful brute!" she spluttered. "I don't like him at all!"

"You met the fairy?"

"Don't be absurd. A fairy would never behave in this barbaric fashion. He's an elf," she fairly spat as she climbed out of the bucket and squeezed the milk out of her wings. "But even so, I can't imagine what's got into him! He's not normal. All I wanted was to ask him a few questions!"

"An elf?" Jake echoed as he handed her a little kitchen hand towel to dry herself off. "Then why has he got a sparkle-trail?"

"Oh, if you go back far enough, fairies, elves, and leprechauns are all different branches of the same family tree," she said impatiently. "Archie's Mr. Darwin would have a field day with that one."

"Gladwin..." Jake waved off her news about the elf, for he had news of his own. "You won't believe what just happened out there. The gingerbread men have come to life, and they're fighting each other!"

She paused in drying herself and frowned at him like he was a loon-bat. "What?"

"The gingerbread display! There's a whole battle going on between Mademoiselle Marie's French courtier cookies and British Bob's ginger-knights from his cookie castle downstairs! They're at each other's throats!"

She stared at him in confusion, then started laughing. "Oh, you almost got me there, you rascal."

"I'm not joking!" But before he could tell her about the gingerbread sweethearts who were apparently eloping together, Jake caught a glimmer of red-and-green sparkles in a dark corner of the kitchen.

He thrust the matter of the gingerbread battle aside, homing in on their quarry. "There," he murmured ever so discreetly to his companions. "I see him. In the corner."

Red's ears pricked up.

"He's spying on us." Jake sidled over to the kitchen door and closed it behind him. Then he locked it so the little miscreant couldn't escape.

Nobody shoved their favorite fairy into a milk pail and got away with it.

Jake glanced at Gladwin. "I trust you have no further objections to me capturing him?"

"Hardly!" She let out another huff. "If he had nothing to hide, he would've answered my questions. Whatever he's doing here, he's obviously up to no good." She tossed the towel aside and flew a few feet up into the air, a little unsteady on her still-drying wings.

Jake nodded at the Gryphon. "C'mon, Red. Let's get him," he whispered. "You grab him, I'll bag him."

Red's golden eyes gleamed in the darkness as he nodded back firmly, eager for the hunt.

CHAPTER FIVE
To Catch an Elf

"**Y**ou might as well give yourself up!" Jake warned the unseen creature lurking in the kitchen. "We know you're in here. We've got you cornered now. We can do this the easy way or the hard way."

"Look out!" Gladwin cried as a cast-iron saucepan came flying out of the darkness at him.

Jake deflected it just in time with his telekinesis; otherwise, it would have hit him squarely in the noggin. He scowled as it clattered to the floor.

"Shh!" Gladwin scolded. "You'll bring the constable running!"

Jake narrowed his eyes in annoyance, scanning the dark kitchen. "Nice try, elf! You missed."

He heard a nasty snicker in response.

"You're only making it worse for yourself!"

"Let's hope he doesn't try throwing any kitchen knives," Gladwin mumbled, then suddenly pointed. "There!"

More red-and-green sparkles appeared, running along the kitchen's top shelf.

By their glow, Jake could just make out a little figure about knee-high, eighteen inches tall or so. He had a pointy red hat with a white pompom on the end, a green coat, and candy-striped stockings above his curly-toed shoes.

But the Christmas elf was blazingly fast, dodging away, as if he could not decide whether it was more fun to torment them a bit more, or if he should just try to get away.

"We only want to talk to you!" Jake lied as he followed the fading sparkle-trail. Dash it, he had already lost sight of the elf. "What are you doing in this shop?" he asked into the darkness. "Shouldn't you be at the North Pole making toys or something?"

"Santa will hear of this!" Gladwin warned. "This is *not* very Christmassy behavior!"

"I hate Christmas!" a small, angry voice retorted.

In that instant, Red homed in on the exact spot where the sound had come from and pounced.

Alas, the Gryphon came up empty and suddenly started coughing. Jake and Gladwin heard another mocking laugh.

Then they smelled cinnamon. Red gagged and coughed, his golden eyes watering.

"Red, are you all right?" Jake hurried over to his pet in concern. When he reached Red's side, he realized the spiteful little elf had just flung a handful of cinnamon into the Gryphon's eyes.

Red sputtered and sneezed, wheezed and coughed, then shook himself, his golden eyes watering and suddenly blazing with indignation, as if to say, *That does it!*

"Oh, you've got it coming now, elf," Jake vowed, pulling the folded up burlap sack out of his coat. He shook it open, giving Red a meaningful nod. "You shouldn't have done that, whoever you are!"

"Caw!" Red coughed again, but he was ready to continue hunting their quarry.

"I don't see him," Jake whispered after a moment. "Where'd he go? He can't have got far."

"Oh, I probably should have mentioned this before." Gladwin flew alongside Jake's shoulder. "But Christmas elves can kind of, well, make themselves almost invisible."

"Oh, great," Jake muttered.

"It's a defense mechanism—you know, so children can't see them around Christmastime. Santa has it, too. But their sparkles still show."

"Santa has a sparkle-trail?"

"A little bit of one, sometimes. He *does* have elven blood, you know. How else would he be able to do all he does without the help of magic?"

Jake frowned. He had no particular regard for Santa Claus, but he'd had no idea that Christmas elves could make themselves invisible. Blimey, what else didn't he know about them? "Can they fly?"

"No, but if they get a running start, they can jump so well that it's almost like flying—over short distances, anyway."

Jake growled under his breath, then had to tell himself to quit getting frustrated. He had battled much more formidable foes than one irksome little elf. Gargoyles, giants, Norse gods, a wicked sea witch, and a power-mad uncle, just to name a few. This should be but child's play for a future Lightrider like him...

He suddenly got an idea.

"Let's block the exits. If he sees he can't get out, maybe he'll give himself up. Gladwin, you hover in front of the lock on the kitchen door and hit him with your fairy dust if he tries to get past you. I'll guard the window. Red, you block the fireplace in case he tries to get out through the chimney."

The others agreed. At once, they split up to man their posts, but the elf must have realized their intent, for there was a flash of red-and-green sparkles as he suddenly went wild, rushing around the kitchen, looking for any weakness.

They held fast.

"He's coming at you, Gladwin!"

She hurled a glob of milk-sopped fairy dust at him. The elf ducked and thus avoided getting hit by its stunning effects, but in the blink of an eye, he tested Jake next.

Jake could barely see the elf, he moved so fast. As the knee-high outline of the small, angry creature came speeding toward him, the sparkle-trail glimmered out behind him like long strands of gift-wrap ribbons stuck to his shoes.

The moonlight streaming in through the window over the sink gave Jake a glimpse of the elf's wizened face, pointy ears, and remarkably big nose. Rushing out of the darkness, already in motion, the elf started to gather himself to jump over Jake's head toward the window.

But Jake was not about to let him pass. He threw up his arms to block him, then remembered at the last minute that he could use his telekinesis to bounce him back.

Pah! He flicked his fingers in the charging elf's direction...

But sometimes, unfortunately, Jake got overexcited in the midst of some adventure, and on such occasions, he tended to use too much strength.

Bam!

The bolt of energy from his telekinesis hit the elf. The little creature yelped, zooming backward through the air. Jake gasped, afraid he had just accidentally killed the little fellow by slamming him too hard against the opposite wall.

Thankfully, Red was already on his way. Mid-pounce, the Gryphon snatched the flying elf in his beak right out of the air, like a big dog catching a ball thrown by his young master.

Rather than being relieved not to have had his neck broken, the elf started kicking and cursing as Red held him up off the ground, dangling him by his little red suspenders.

Jake rushed over, opening the gunnysack wide as he ran; Red dropped the elf into the sack and Jake instantly closed it, knotting up its rough twine ties.

"Got you! Good catch, Red," Jake said, even as the elf began thrashing about in the sack, unable to escape.

"Let me out!"

Jake lifted the sack higher and spoke to it. "Be still, you little pest! You've got no business in this bakery. I know it was you who got me thrown out of here today for knocking over the creampuff tree. More importantly, I want to know how you brought those gingerbread folk to life! How'd you do it?"

The thrashing paused. Another smug snicker emerged from inside the burlap sack.

Jake fumed.

"You see how rude he is?" Gladwin exclaimed.

Red, meanwhile, still smelled like cinnamon.

"Let's get out of here," Jake grumbled.

Carrying the sack in one hand, he unlocked the kitchen door with the other. As he opened it to let the other two go ahead of him, he glanced over his shoulder with a slight twinge of guilt at the mess they had left in Marie's formerly tidy kitchen. She'd likely blame Bob for it somehow, based on what he'd seen, Jake thought.

He wondered what had happened between the two bakers.

Just as he and his companions headed for the shop's front door, Archie opened it and poked his head in, beckoning anxiously. "Hurry! We've got company! Night watchman's coming down the street!"

"Gladwin, can't you turn off those sparkles?" Jake whispered at once. "What if the bobby sees the light? You're going to get us caught!"

"I can't help it! They only stop if I stop flying. Oh, never mind. Just go. I'll wait in here and hide until the bobby passes. I won't let him see me. You two go on. I'll catch up later. Maybe I'll tidy up the kitchen a bit. I feel rather bad about the mess."

"Have a look at the gingerbread battle while you're waiting. There were two cookies that escaped."

"Jake, hurry!" Archie called in a loud whisper. "He's coming!"

"Go!" Gladwin urged, shooing them away before hunkering down on a shelf to avoid leaving a sparkle-trail, which would surely draw the bobby's eye when he came strolling down the street on the night watch.

Red pounced out of the shop and Archie quickly climbed onto his back. Jake pulled the bakery door shut silently, then joined his frantic cousin.

Holding on to Red's collar with one hand and clutching the gunnysack with the elf in the other, he mumbled that he was ready.

Red took a few graceful running strides down the cobbled lane, and then lifted off with a whoosh of his powerful wings.

It was fortunate that the night was dark enough that the bobby didn't see them flying away into the starry, black sky.

The curious constable did, however, pause in front of the bakery. He bent down, wondering what sort of dog breed could have left such large paw prints in the snow. Irish wolfhound, perhaps?

"Hmm!" he said to himself before shrugging off the question and moving on with his patrol, continually scanning the darkness.

After all, crime never slept.

CHAPTER SIX
We Have Ways To Make You Talk

After their windy ride through the frigid night skies, Jake was glad when their destination came into view below: the broad, snowy roofs and turrets of Beacon House, crowned by its great lantern glowing in the darkness from inside the center cupola.

The tree-shaped symbol silhouetted in the glass was a signal of safe haven to all magical creatures in the area.

And so it was.

For the old, rambling Tudor mansion beside the River Thames had long been the headquarters of the Order of the Yew Tree, a secret alliance sworn to keeping the balance between the magical and non-magical peoples of the earth.

Jake's parents had been among the Order's elite agents known as Lightriders, while Archie and Isabelle's parents, Lord and Lady Bradford, served in a tamer capacity as diplomats.

They were frequently away, sent off to distant corners of the sprawling British Empire to smooth out quarrels between magic and non-magic folk. (Currently they were in the Near East sorting out some sort of misunderstanding with the djinnis.)

That was why Archie and Isabelle were so frequently left in the care of their tutor and governess, Henry and Helena, and overseen by Great-Great Aunt Ramona, who, herself, was an Elder of the Order.

But it was just as well that Lord and Lady Bradford were away, Jake thought. He wasn't sure what his aunt and uncle would have thought about his dragging Archie along on this mission to break into the bakery and abduct the troublemaker elf.

The little miscreant was still flailing around inside the gunnysack. Jake clutched it tightly in his half-frozen hands while Red glided to a smooth halt on a flat stretch of the old mansion's roof.

"F-f-finally!" Archie said, his teeth chattering. "M-m-maybe M-M-Mrs. Appleton will make us some n-nice, hot t-t-t-tea."

The elf must have realized they had come to a halt, for he chose that moment to switch his tactics. "Help! Help! I'm being kidnapped!" he shouted from inside the sack.

"Not kidnapped—arrested, you dolt," Jake said. "Stop kicking me!" He swung off his Gryphon after Archie had dismounted and gave the sack a stern shake. "Behave yourself in there! We are not going to hurt you!"

The elf blew raspberries at him in response.

"Charming," Jake muttered.

"Becaw," Red said, nodding at his cozy aerie in a sheltered corner of the roof.

Jake nodded. "All right, we'll call you if we need you, boy. Thanks for your help."

While Red went to curl up in his nest, Jake carried the gunnysack over to the little door on the center cupola that housed the great lantern. Narrowing his eyes a bit against the light's golden glow, he opened the door and stepped inside. Archie followed, his spectacles instantly fogging up.

Warmed by the beacon's glass-enclosed flame, both boys sighed with relief as the welcoming heat infused them. Then they started down the tight spiral stairs that led into the rest of the house.

At the bottom of the stairs, they stepped out of a closet-like door into an upstairs hallway. Not stopping here, they marched on, past the long row of bedchambers, until they reached the top of the grand staircase.

The wide, ornately carved stairway overlooked the foyer and led to the main rooms of the Order's mansion headquarters.

"Oh, look," Archie said, pointing into the foyer below them. "They've put up a Christmas tree."

The plump, rosy-cheeked housekeeper must have heard them coming, for she came hurrying out from the vicinity of the kitchens just then. "My dear boys!" she greeted them with a wreath of smiles. "It's so nice to see you! Oh, but I'm afraid Guardian Stone isn't here right now. Didn't he tell you he's gone to visit his mother for the holidays?"

"Oh, yes, we know, Mrs. Appleton," Archie said. "We're not here to see Derek. We're here on *business*," he added proudly.

Jake shot him a glance that warned him not to say too much. "Could we use the library, please?"

"Of course! Make yourselves at home. You young gentlemen are always welcome here." She beamed as they trudged down the steps. "Such rosy cheeks, and all the shivering! Why, you look like you could do with some tea."

"Ah, Mrs. Appleton! You must have some house brownie blood in your veins."

She beamed at the compliment on her housekeeping skills. "Actually, I am one-sixteenth house brownie, on me mother's side."

"I thought so," Archie said sweetly, trying to distract her from the small *"Help!"* that came from inside the thrashing burlap sack that dangled from Jake's grasp.

"But, er, what have you got there, young masters?"

"Never you mind, Mrs. Appleton," Jake drawled. He flashed a breezy grin as they passed her, determined to brazen it out. He might be only twelve, but he was still an earl, after all. No servant in her right mind would ever question a future peer of the realm.

At least he hoped not.

The boys crossed the foyer, trying to look nonchalant, but when they gained the library and shut the door behind them, they exchanged a glance of relief.

Eager to get down to business, they strode into the enchanted library of Beacon House, with its floor-to-ceiling bookshelves, its rolling ladder, and red velvet drapes. The portrait of Queen Elizabeth in silver armor stared down from above the fireplace with the wreck of the Spanish Armada in the background.

In the far corner, the mysterious lighted globe revealed the locations of the Order's many Lightriders out on their various missions, and to the left, displayed proudly on its pedestal, the magic harp played Christmas carols softly to itself.

"Would you see if there's a wand I could borrow over there?" Jake nodded at the large, stately desk to his right.

Archie nodded, drawing off his gloves.

While Jake set the gunnysack with his prisoner on one of the brown leather club chairs, his cousin marched over to the desk and started rummaging around amid the brightly colored ribbons and crepe paper left behind from somebody's gift-wrapping project, probably Mrs. Appleton's.

While Jake unwound his red scarf from around his neck, grateful for the cheerful fire burning in the hearth, Archie said hello to the Inkbug when it came trundling out of its box to see what was going on.

"Any luck?" Jake asked his cousin.

"Not yet. Is there a wand in here?" Archie asked the furry little caterpillar.

At once, the helpful insect ran across the inkpad to get ink on its many feet. Then it ran back and forth across an open pad of notepaper and printed out the answer: *Second drawer.*

"Thanks. Ah, here it is!" Archie quickly found the crooked yew wand and nodded his thanks to the creature, then he brought the ordinary-looking twig over to Jake. "What are you going to do to him? You don't really know that many spells."

Jake shushed him with a reproachful scowl. "Yes, but he doesn't know that," he whispered, barely mouthing the words. *It's called a bluff, you idiot.*

Oh, right! Archie mouthed back. Honest to a fault, the boy genius gave him a conspiratorial wink, finally catching on.

Jake shook his head. Good egg, Archie, but the perfect little English gentleman wouldn't have lasted a day in the rookery. He gripped the wand. "Maybe I should try that spell on him that I used in Wales to turn those living gargoyles back into stone?" Jake suggested loud enough for the elf to hear.

"Oh, not that one, Jake, it's too terrible!" Archie said in a convincing tone of dread, playing along. Then he addressed their prisoner. "Whoever you are, I'd do as he says, if I were you."

"I'm not afraid of you two runts!" the elf retorted from inside the brown sack.

Archie frowned. "What a rudesby."

Jake's frown deepened. He beckoned his cousin aside for a private word. "We need to question him, but we've got to figure out some way to keep him under control before we dare untie the sack. Otherwise, he'll escape. It was hard enough catching him the first time."

"Hmm." Archie glanced around in thought. "Hey! Why don't we just tie him up with all those gift-wrap ribbons?"

"You *are* brilliant," Jake admitted. Archie clapped him on the shoulder and ran over to the desk to get them.

Attempting to bind the elf's wrists and ankles would have required them to open the sack. That would only have made it easier for the elf to escape. So, instead, the boys simply wrapped the ribbons around and around the elf's squirmy body, sack and all, piling on layer after layer, as if they were wrapping up a Christmas-colored mummy.

Finally, when the elf could do no more than wiggle his toes inside his curly shoes and thrash his head from side to side in angry protest, they untied the knot sealing the gunnysack and peeled it down enough to let their prisoner poke his head out.

The little elf glared at them.

Jake couldn't help smiling at his disgruntled stare. "Now you'll answer our questions."

The harp played on all the while; the elf glanced past the boys, scowling at it, as he took in his surroundings. "What do you want with me, you kidnappers? You've got no right abducting me! I have rights!"

"That remains to be seen," Jake replied. "What were you doing in that bakery?"

"And why did you try to attack us back there?" Archie chimed in. "You could've just spoken to us like a civilized person. I had no idea Christmas elves could be so vicious."

"Christmas!" the elf said in disgust. "Bah! Shoddiest holiday on the calendar. They should do away with it altogether! I'm no Christmas elf. Not anymore. Not ever! Would you *please* shut that thing up?" The elf glared past them at the magic harp.

"Oh, you don't like music?" Jake sent Archie a smug glance as they realized their prisoner's weakness. "I have a better idea." He leaned closer with a threatening stare. "You explain yourself right now, or I'll make the harp play louder. Who are you?"

"Humbug!"

"You'd better answer me," Jake warned.

"I just told you!"

"Humbug is your name?"

"Well, it suits him, to be sure," Archie muttered.

"What did you do to those gingerbread men? We know it was you who made the displays come alive. How did you manage that?"

"None of your business," Humbug answered grandly.

"I see," Jake said. "Harp, play louder, please. Something to get us into the Christmas spirit."

"No! Not Christmas carols! Anything but that!" Humbug cried.

The harp ignored him, launching into a jaunty rendition of "Good King Wenceslas."

Jake and Archie sang along just to be annoying.

The angry elf blustered and huffed, his feet kicking, but his arms were stuck at his sides, thanks to his brightly colored bindings, and he could not cover his ears.

"Feel like talking yet?" Jake asked.

Humbug's only answer was more raspberries.

"Let's hear another one, harp!"

It obeyed with glee. They sang along.

"Deck the halls with boughs of holly..."

"Noooo!"

"Fa, la, la, la, la, la..." Jake clapped his hands in time while Archie sang along, strolling over to the library card catalogue as he did so.

Archie opened the little rectangular drawer marked "E" and started searching alphabetically for any information or recent news filed under *Elves*.

"Don we now..."

"Oh, stop, stop—for pity's sake, no! I can't take any more!"

"I'll stop the music if you'll stop lying," Jake said pleasantly, feeling rather pleased so far with his own interrogation skills.

Of course, having been arrested numerous times in his pickpocket days, he had learned from the best—like Constable Flanagan—when he had been on the receiving end.

"Harp, pause," Jake ordered. "That will do, for the moment." He turned back to Humbug. "I mean, you can't deny you are a Christmas elf, for starters. Look at you. Look at your clothes. What else could you possibly be, dressed like that? Besides, we clearly saw your sparkle-trail. It was red-and-green. Red and green equals Christmas."

"I am a *Halloween* elf!" Humbug thundered in fury.

Jake's eyebrows shot upward at this announcement.

Archie turned around from the catalogue drawer. "Who ever heard of a Halloween elf? There's no such thing."

"I will be the first!" the angry elf declared.

"Come again?" Jake demanded.

Humbug pursed his mouth with a stubborn glare.

"I see. Still not ready to talk, eh? I'm afraid you leave me no choice. Harp?"

The enchanted instrument waited eagerly for his next request.

Jake narrowed his eyes at Humbug. Time to get serious. "Play 'Jingle Bells.'"

It did.

The elf howled in protest, thrashing his head from side to side, kicking his little feet, to no avail. "Oh, make it stop! No more, please, I beg you! Anything but that!"

"No...mercy." Jake held up his hand to stop his cousin from responding to the elf's piteous pleas.

Archie looked worried, but Jake refused to fall for Humbug's deceptions. He had to make his point.

Humbug howled in fury (or possibly annoyance to the point of pain) at having to listen to "Jingle Bells" for probably the twenty-thousandth time in his life.

With all the fuss the elf was making, even the Inkbug grew concerned. The fuzzy little caterpillar crept out of its box once more and stared at their beribboned captive, its little antennae cocked in alarm.

"Jake!" Archie pointed at the Inkbug as the little caterpillar decided to intervene on the prisoner's behalf. It started scuttling back and forth across the inkpad, spelling out a message: *Stop! You're torturing him!*

"Oh, he's fine," Jake told the insect, but the Inkbug reared up on its hind legs and shook its upper parts, *No.* It ran back and forth along the notepad again and spelled out another message: *Stop it now or I'll send a message to your aunt!*

"Oh, no, you won't," Jake warned.

It started twitching its antennae to tattletale on him. Before it could telegraph its message to Aunt Ramona's Inkbug on the receiving end, Jake picked up the caterpillar and gave it a stern look. "You stay out of this! That elf may be small, but he's caused a lot of trouble. He attacked Gladwin!"

The Inkbug drew back, looking shocked at this revelation. Then it, too, scowled at Humbug.

At that moment, thankfully, the stubborn elf submitted. "Oh, very well! Please, I give up! I'll tell you everything! Just make that horrid music stop! Please, no more carols! I can't bear it anymore!"

"Harp, silence," Jake ordered with a smile.

CHAPTER SEVEN
Jingle Bells

The magic harp quit playing, mid-bar. Jake set the Inkbug down on the desk, then marched back to the chair, where the ribbon-swathed Humbug sat groaning.

"Ugh, you have no idea what it's like hearing those same songs day after day after day, year round, summer, spring, autumn. It's enough to drive me mad!"

"Apparently, it has." Jake leaned his hips back against the desk opposite their captive and arched a brow. "I'm sorry to have to tell you this, but there's no such thing as a Halloween elf. So, what's all this about?"

"Oh, I hate Christmas, if you must know! I never asked to be born an elf! I'm done with all of it, I tell you. All that happy holiday cheer. Ugh!" Humbug shuddered in spite of his bindings. "What's everybody so happy about, anyway? Presents? Bah! Nobody ever gave *me* anything. Just a lot of headaches. Mix that batter, clean those pots, decorate those cookies. 'Yes, Mrs. Claus. Right away, Mrs. Claus.' Blah, blah, blah, blah, blah. It never ends!"

"I thought Christmas elves make toys," Jake said.

"I work for the missus," he grumbled.

"Mrs. Claus?" Archie asked.

"That's right. Pair of tyrants, those two. The Clauses. They've made all of us elves their slaves, but contrary to myth, there are many different jobs we're forced to do."

"Forced?" Archie asked. "I thought your kind volunteered for their positions."

Humbug scoffed. "Oh, you two are naïve. Who'd voluntarily want to live in the North Pole? Honestly! Not that we get any credit for all our pains." The elf huffed. "As if he could pull it off without us! Christmas is more complicated than you can possibly imagine, but he gets all the credit—while we do all the work! Elves do everything for Santa. From the secretaries, who keep the Nice and Naughty lists, to the poor fools who muck out the awful, smelly reindeer stalls.

"It's true that scores of my kind work in Santa's sweatshops, building toys. Me, I worked in Mrs. Claus's Christmas kitchens. Baking treats for all the good little boys and girls," he mimicked with a sneer.

"Is that why you were in Mademoiselle Marie's bakery? Don't even try to tell me you were only there to help her."

"Please," Humbug said with a sarcastic snort. "No, you runt—"

"Don't call me that!" Jake snapped.

"Well, I don't know what else to call you!" Humbug snapped. "You never mentioned your name *when you were abducting me!*"

"I am Jake, the Earl of Griffon, and that's my cousin Archie."

"Oh, really? Earl of Griffon, eh?" Humbug eyed him in suspicion, but he looked like he recognized the name.

"Well?" Jake persisted. "Why were you in that bakery?"

Humbug looked away. "Not that it's any of your business, but I don't want to work for the Clauses anymore. I want to work in Halloween Town! Oh, go on, laugh. I don't care. I'm going to prove I'm perfect for the Halloween job by ruining Christmas for as many of these cheerful London idiots as possible. Like you! Ha, ha, you should've seen your face when I knocked over the *Croquembouche* and you got the blame for it! Ha, ha, ha!"

Jake refused to rise to the bait of his taunting. "Why do you want to ruin Christmas?"

"I'm on a mission for Cap'n Jack," the wizened little elf said with great self-importance.

"Jack who?"

"Jack O'Lantern, if you must know! Now there's a proper ruler of a holiday for you. He goes by many names. The Great Scarecrow, Old Turnip Head. Lord Samhain himself!"

"Turnip head?" Jake echoed in a quizzical tone.

Archie looked at him and shrugged.

Jake knew that, for centuries, children throughout the British Isles had hollowed out turnips to use as jack-o-lanterns on Halloween night. He'd heard that in America they used some strange, native gourd called a pumpkin for this purpose, but everyone knew a proper jack-o-lantern was a hollowed-out turnip with a candle stub burning inside it, and had been, for time immemorial.

Humbug was looking at him strangely.

"What?" Jake prompted.

"Oh, nothing. It's just...Cap'n Jack is well aware of you, the boy with the Gryphon."

"Me?" Jake was rather alarmed by this revelation. He was not sure he wanted the lord of Halloween bothering about him.

"Oh, yes," Humbug murmured, eyeing him from head to toe in scorn. "The famous Lightriders' son."

"I can't imagine why he should be interested in me."

"Think about it. The Great Scarecrow has got whole brigades of ghosts at his bidding, and you're one of the few people who can see 'em. He worries you could be a problem someday. Warns his ghosts to steer clear of you when they fly out at night to do their mischief, haunting old castles, causing nightmares, and such."

"I see," Jake said warily.

"The whole underworld knows who you are. I should know. I just came from there a week ago."

"What were you doing there?"

"Looking for a new job, like I told you." Humbug hesitated. "As you pointed out, nobody's ever heard of a Halloween elf, so the Great Scarecrow wasn't sure if he wanted to hire me or not." Humbug shrugged. "But he said he'd give me a chance to prove myself. A test, to see if I was really cut out for good, honest, Halloween work."

"And just what might that entail?" Jake drawled.

"You know, running amuck, pulling pranks, scaring people. That sort of thing."

"So that's what you were doing in that bakery."

"Aye!" Humbug said. "The Great Scarecrow gave me a shaker of Spiteful Spice to sprinkle into the bakers' dough." The elf let out a diabolical laugh. "*Finally,* I get the chance to put people in a bad mood instead of spreading idiotic holiday cheer."

"So that's why those sweets made us feel so awful!" Archie said.

"Did you eat a lot of them? Ha, ha, ha! Most fun I ever had!" Humbug laughed harder. "Bringing the gingerbread displays to life, well, that was just my own little, magical holiday touch. How was I to know they'd start trying to kill each other as soon as they came to life? Ha, ha! What a shame! Probably because they were made by two people who can't stand each other."

"Did you cause the quarrel between Marie and Bob, too?" Jake demanded.

"Hardly!" Humbug couldn't resist snickering again. "But I did my best to help it along. Such fun! Old Turnip-Head is going to love having an ex-Christmas elf as his right-hand man, organizing things. The Clauses run a tight ship, I can tell you.

"They taught me excellent management skills—how to run a workshop, all of it. Those ghosts and ghouls have no idea what it's like to really work for a living. All they have to do is hang around a cemetery groaning and moaning, clank a few chains.

"One night a year they have their duties, while Christmas takes months of preparation! It's busy as a beehive at the North Pole from October through Twelfth Night. Well, once I'm on the Halloween staff, they're going to find out what it's like to run a proper holiday!

"Now, if you're quite through interviewing me, you runts, I demand you release me from these ropes and let me get on with my life. You have no right to hold me here."

"Set you free, so you can go back to ruining people's Christmases? I don't think so," Jake replied, folding his arms across his chest.

"Hullo," Archie suddenly murmured, still poring over the enchanted library's card catalogue. He glanced at Jake. "I think I've found something on our little friend here."

"Who you calling little?" Humbug challenged him.

Archie ignored him, pulling a small white card out of the library drawer. He walked away, following the information on the card; it guided him to one of the lower bookshelves, where he searched until he found a large bound volume of newspapers several weeks old.

The front cover was labeled "October." He flipped open the collection of outdated newspapers, glancing once more at the card to find the page in question. "Here."

"What is it?" Jake asked.

"A missing persons report. This is from a notice that appeared in the *Clairvoyant*. That's the main newspaper that covers magical affairs." Then Archie read aloud from the entry: "'Santa Claus, a.k.a. Kris Kringle, Father Christmas, Jolly Old St. Nick, etc. came in personally to file a report on one of his kitchen elves, called Humbug, who disappeared from his compound in the North Pole on October the tenth. Mrs. Claus is distraught for her little helper's safety. Anyone with information on Humbug's whereabouts should report to Beacon House.'"

"Well, well, how about that?" Jake smirked at the elf. "You might despise the Clauses, but they seem genuinely worried about you."

Humbug rolled his eyes. "Bloody do-gooders."

"So, you just ran away, then? You quit your job without even letting them know? They were probably worried that you froze to death."

"That's not all," Archie continued. "According to this, Santa's offering a reward for Humbug's safe return."

Jake looked over sharply. "What kind of reward?"

Archie read from the paper: "One Christmas wish granted, courtesy of Santa."

"Is that so?" Jake's eyes glazed over at the possibilities.

Humbug looked at him in alarm.

"I want that," Jake murmured all of a sudden.

Archie furrowed his brow. "Coz, you own a goldmine. What could you possibly need that you don't already have the money to buy?"

Jake stared at him for a long moment, remembering all those awful Christmases at the orphanage. "There are some things money can't buy, Arch. Sorry, Humbug. You're going back to Santa."

"Nooooo!"

A knock at the library door just then proved to be Mrs. Appleton bringing them their tea.

Jake hurried to get the door and took the tray from her with profuse thanks, blocking the dear old housekeeper from getting a look into the room at their prisoner.

Best to avoid questions.

He stood in the doorway and took the tray from her. As he hurried her off again with a taut smile, Gladwin arrived through the small fairy door cut high into the front wall of the foyer.

It was well disguised by a carved curlicue in the decorative woodwork, but it allowed all fairies to come and go from Beacon House at will.

Flying down from the fairy door, past the chandelier, Gladwin hurried to join the boys in the library.

"Perfect timing," Jake greeted her. "I trust everything went all right with the bobby?" he asked once Mrs. Appleton was out of earshot.

Gladwin nodded. "He never even noticed me. And I was able to tidy up Marie's shop a bit before I left."

"That was nice of you." As Jake shut the library door again and carried the tray of steaming hot tea and Scottish shortbread in to share with his cousin, he caught Gladwin up on the information they had extracted from the elf and the missing persons report.

Gladwin narrowed her eyes at Humbug. "Halloween Town? Why would you want to work among that rabble? You're an elf, for goodness' sake. What, you'd rather be a goblin?"

"He acts like one," Archie muttered.

"I don't expect you or anyone else to understand," Humbug said. "Everyone thinks that Santa's such a saint—"

"Well, he is, actually," Archie pointed out. "*Saint* Nick. Do you even realize how ungrateful you sound? I'm tired of hearing you tear down Santa and Mrs. Claus. Most people around the world love them dearly, you know. Think of all they do for others!"

While Archie proceeded to scold Humbug, Jake turned to Gladwin. "I hate to ask this of you since you only just arrived, but we don't have much time. I need another favor."

She sighed. "What now?"

"Would you fly back to my house and tell the girls to get over here? They're not going to want to miss this."

"Miss what?" Archie asked.

Jake grinned at his cousin. "We're going to the North Pole."

"Really?" Gladwin asked in surprise.

"Er, except for one minor problem," Archie pointed out. "We don't know the way. I mean, obviously, we head north, but the North Pole is somewhere in the middle of the Arctic. From what I understand, Santa's compound is very well hidden."

"So?"

"So, if we get lost up there, we're dead."

"He knows the way." Jake nodded at their captive.

The elf snorted. "What makes you think I'll cooperate?"

Jake leaned closer and looked him in the eyes. "Because if you don't, I'll feed you to my Gryphon." Then he gave the elf a hard look, took another gulp of tea, and headed for the door. "Watch him, Archie. I'll be back soon."

"Where are you going?"

"To arrange our transportation."

"Well, I guess it's back out into the cold for me," Gladwin said. "I'm off to fetch the girls."

"Tell them to hurry and dress warm. Say, before you go..." Jake paused. "Could I borrow some of your fairy dust?"

She looked at him in surprise. "Whatever for?"

"It makes things fly, right?"

She nodded. "It can do that." She handed him the tiny pouch of fairy dust she carried with her. It was no larger than a single green pea. "You won't do anything rash with it, will you?"

"Who, me?" He grinned. "So, will you be coming with us?"

"To the North Pole? Can't possibly. Too busy." She shook her head in regret. "I've got stacks of Christmas cards to deliver for the Queen."

It was disappointing news, but Jake nodded, well aware that Gladwin took her duties as a royal fairy courier very seriously.

"You be careful," she warned. "The North Pole's a long way off, with many dangers."

"I've got Risker with me." He patted his magic dagger, sheathed at his side. "And we'll have Red to look after us, too. Don't worry, we'll be back in plenty of time for me to glue that ridiculous beard to my chin for the Nativity play."

Gladwin chuckled. "I'll see you there, then. I have a starring role in it myself, you know."

"You do? What about the audience? I thought ordinary folk aren't allowed to see the fairies. But you're going to be in the play? As what?"

"You'll see." She bade him farewell with a familiar, teasing tug on his blond forelock, then flew up to the tiny, hidden door.

"Hmm." Jake shrugged off this entertaining mystery and headed down the central hallway, letting himself out the back door.

He stepped out onto the frosty terrace, then marched across the snow-dusted garden to the carriage house, which sat by the stables behind the mansion.

Inside the dark carriage house, he passed a collection of fine coaches and servant wagons belonging to the Order, most of which possessed hidden magical qualities. He stopped when he came to the large open sleigh. "Perfect."

They won't mind if I borrow this for a day or two.

He hauled open the wide door across from it, and started trying to drag the sleigh outside by its jingle-bell-studded harness.

It did not want to come.

The sled-like runners scraped stubbornly across the flagstone floor. He struggled to get it outside, first pulling it as best he could, and then pushing the vehicle from behind with all his strength.

Blast, this thing's heavy! he thought, annoyed, until it dawned on him to use his telekinesis. He rolled his eyes at himself. Would he never get used to having magical powers?

Lifting his hands from his sides, Jake concentrated hard on the sleigh and managed to lift its sturdy bulk off the coach-house floor. Using nothing but his mind, he made it glide through the air, out of the carriage house, into the starlight. Then he set it down gently on the snow.

He dragged the wide door shut again, then lifted his gaze up to the roof of Beacon House and let out a loud whistle.

A moment later, Red peeked over the edge of the roof, leaving his cozy eagle's nest in answer to the summons.

Jake beckoned him down.

The Gryphon leaped off the rooftop and started circling his way down amid the tall, bare garden trees. Meanwhile, Jake took out Gladwin's tiny pouch of fairy dust and wondered if it would be enough.

Though there was only a pinch of it, he sprinkled it all over the sleigh. To his amazement, the vehicle lifted off the ground and hovered in midair.

An eager smile spread across his face as he stared at it.

With all the holiday preparations going on, this was most unexpected, but suddenly, his anticipation for a new adventure was rushing through his veins.

"Becaw?" Red asked, tilting his head in puzzlement when he landed and saw the floating sleigh.

Jake grinned at his pet. "I know you're a royal Gryphon and all, boy, but tell me. How do you feel about pulling a sleigh?"

Red's feathery eyebrows drew together in a dubious stare as Jake held up the leather harness and gave its jingle bells a jaunty shake.

CHAPTER EIGHT
Yetis

B efore long, all four kids sat in the sleigh as it soared through a dark indigo sky spangled with stars. Though the night was bitter cold, the enchanted sleigh enveloped them in a magical bubble of warmth, thanks to some Order spell built into it.

Their cheeks were rosy, and their eyes smarted every now and then when a burst of wintry wind blew by. But bundled up in several layers of warm clothes, they were quite comfortable.

They stared down over the edges of the vehicle, marveling at the miles of frosted patchwork countryside beneath them.

With every powerful beat of Red's wings, they traversed England, heading ever northward. They saw a train chugging through the hills. It looked no larger than a toy.

Before long, they passed over the dark moorlands of the North Country; next the Scottish Highlands rose, reaching for the moon; soon it was time to venture out over the frigid North Sea.

They passed above the windy Scottish isles where the wild ponies roamed. Across the water lay the shores of the old Viking homelands they had visited a few months ago, Norway and the other Scandinavian countries.

Jake drove the magic sleigh ever northward, until the land disappeared entirely, and the cold sea was a black, watery blanket waving beneath them.

Soon, the distant white edge of Greenland came into sight—or was it the Arctic? Jake hardly knew.

He was just glad he had worn thick wool mittens as a second layer over his gloves. Otherwise, his hands might have frozen to the reins, even in spite of the sleigh's magic spell. It was indeed frigid in these climes, but their excitement to meet Santa in person kept them warm.

Of course, Dani said she didn't see why Jake should be the one to collect the Christmas wish, since all four of them were returning Humbug to the North Pole together.

Jake insisted, in turn, that it was *his* plan and his Gryphon pulling the floating sleigh. Plus he was the one who had marshaled up the plot to capture the angry elf in the first place; therefore, he should get the wish.

He would not tell the others what he intended to wish for. He already knew what he wanted, but he worried that saying it out loud might cancel it out somehow. You never could tell with wishes. He wasn't taking any chances.

They wondered aloud and chatted together about what Santa would be like in person, while their grumpy little prisoner sat scowling in their midst.

Only Humbug looked indifferent to the cold.

He was no longer wrapped entirely in ribbons like a Christmas mummy, for with further threats of carols on the harp, they had managed to tie him up in a more convenient fashion. Now, only his wrists were bound; it seemed more humane. They had no desire to be cruel to him. It was nearly Christmas, after all.

Besides, they were in a flying sleigh hundreds of feet above the ground. Where could he really go?

What none of the kids realized was that his lighter bindings made it easier for Humbug to reach with his little hand discreetly into his waistcoat and grasp the black satin pouch hidden in his vest pocket.

Nobody noticed what mischief he was up to until the elf suddenly let out a large sneeze.

"Bless you," Dani said automatically.

"Hey, what's all this?" Archie exclaimed.

Humbug cackled.

Jake, driving, looked over his shoulder in question, even as a sharp, spicy smell filled the air.

A cloud of orange glitter hung in their midst, as if it had just come out of Humbug's nose...

Jake's eyes widened as he realized Humbug had just thrown the last of his Spiteful Spice all over them. "You didn't!"

"Oh yes I did!" the elf said with glee.

Oh no.

Spiteful Spice had got in everybody's hair and stuck to their coats.

"Ew, what just came out of your nose? That's disgusting," Isabelle said with a grimace, brushing it off herself.

"What is all this?" Dani asked, quickly doing the same.

Jake had no sooner told the others what the elf had just done when the Spiteful Spice began to take effect.

Isabelle looked at Humbug in outrage. "How dare you?"

"Let's throw him overboard!" Archie yelled.

"No, don't be a dolt, I want that wish!" Jake retorted.

Dani turned on him. "This is your fault! You should have tied him up better!"

"Don't look at me! I'm driving! You lot were supposed to watch him."

"Oh, so this is our fault?" Dani shouted.

Humbug laughed heartily, relishing their instant annoyance at each other. The bickering continued about whose fault it was.

"Never mind! Let's just get this over with," Jake muttered, cracking the whip a little too hard over Red, which the Gryphon did not appreciate at all.

"Caw!"

"Why are we even doing this? This is stupid! I'm cold!" Dani complained.

"Quit whining," Jake ordered.

"Don't tell me what to do!" she thundered. "If you're going to hog the wish all to yourself—as usual—we should've let you do it alone. You're always dragging us into trouble!"

"Am not. I didn't force anybody to come! You came because you wanted to."

"Well, I want to go back now." Dani folded her arms across her chest and glowered.

"Too bad. We're over the middle of the ocean, stupid carrot-head. You're goin' to have to wait."

"Boys and their hare-brained ideas." She shook her head in disgust.

"Hang on, but some boys happen to have lots of good ideas," Archie protested. "Not that anybody ever listens!"

"Oh, the girls listen, Arch. They're just too thick to understand,"

Jake drawled, baiting the redhead.

"Lud, Jake, you're such a boor!" Isabelle suddenly burst out.

All three turned to her, astonished.

It seemed not even the virtuous nature of the Keeper of the Unicorns could withstand the Halloween lord's Spiteful Spice.

She gasped at her own ill-tempered words, and covered her mouth with her hands for a second. "I'm sorry, coz! I-I didn't mean that."

"Well, he is," Dani drawled, looking very pleased that Isabelle agreed with her.

"Ha, ha, ha!" Humbug snickered. "This is so entertaining!"

"You think so?" Turning without warning, Dani hauled off and punched the elf in the nose.

"Are you crazy, you Irish heathen?" Archie yelled at her. Now even the civility of the perfect young English gentleman was starting to fray. "What's Santa going to say if we return the elf with a black eye?"

"When I'm mad, I punch somebody," Dani O'Dell said, lifting her fist in his direction. "You got a problem with that, four eyes?"

"Egads!" Archie said with a lordly huff. "I see you can take the girl out of the rookery, but apparently, you can't take the rookery out of the girl."

"What's that supposed to mean? You think you're so smart, absentminded professor? You'd forget where you put your head if it wasn't attached!"

"Would both of you just shut up?" Isabelle growled at the younger pair.

Jake started laughing (not in a nice way) at Isabelle.

She pointed at him. "Stifle it, Jake! I've had about enough of you!"

"Caw, caw, *becaw!*"

"Don't tell me what to do, you arrogant Gryphon!" Isabelle snapped.

"What did Red say?" Dani demanded.

Isabelle glared. "He told us all to sit down and shut up."

"Somebody had to say it," Humbug muttered.

"Did Red get Spiteful Spice on him, too?" Archie asked. "I just want to know if your Gryphon's going to start ripping us limb from limb."

"Of course not," Jake muttered. "It's just typical Red—oh, excuse me, mighty Claw the Courageous—always thinking he's in charge of everything. Keep going, Red! I said, keep going! Just mind your own business up there and keep flying!"

Red shot Jake a glare over his winged shoulder, as if to say, *"How dare you?"*

Humbug howled with laughter. But the Gryphon, fed up with their behavior, started taking them down reproachfully toward the ground.

"What are you doing?" Jake demanded. "Red, fly! Up! I said, *up*!"

His pet angrily ignored him. With a jangle of his harness, Red landed in an arctic snowfield near a pine forest somewhere in the snowy middle of nowhere.

"I didn't tell you to stop!" Jake yelled.

In answer, Red turned around and gave them all a loud, long lion roar.

The kids' eyes widened and the fringe of each one's hair that showed under their hats blew back a bit.

The Gryphon's ferocious order to his passengers needed no translation: *Behave!*

It got very quiet.

Nobody said anything for a long moment. Finally, Jake growled under his breath, looped the leather reins over their brass holder, and then jumped out of the sleigh to try to clear his head.

The other three climbed out, too, bickering nonstop.

Humbug did something strange, however.

The elf hopped up on the back of the seat and started making the most bizarre noises, a rhythmic staccato of loud, ape-like bellows. He aimed these calls in the direction of the distant tree-line.

Archie left off quarreling with the girls and spun to face him. "What on earth are you doing, you daft little menace?"

Humbug ignored him and continued with the ruckus.

"Stop that!" Jake clenched his jaw in anger and marched back toward the sleigh, crunching across the frozen top layer of the deep snow. "Everybody, shut it for a minute! Humbug, stop making that obnoxious racket! I know you're up to something—"

At that moment, a deep, guttural roar came from the direction of the snowy forest, cutting off his words.

With a collective gasp, they all turned toward the bloodcurdling sound.

They stood motionless for a second, listening.

It had faded away. Now the silence was profound.

"What was that?" Dani breathed.

Jake's heart pounded. He shook his head. "I don't know."

"Look!" Archie suddenly pointed toward the tree-line.

"Happy Christmas, you numskulls!" Humbug snickered. His hands still bound in front of him, the elf leaped off the side of the sleigh, broke through the frozen top layer with a crunch, and disappeared under the deep snow.

He immediately started tunneling away at great speeds, but neither Jake nor any of his companions wasted time going after the elf. They had bigger problems.

Literally.

Three towering figures covered in mangy white fur stepped out from behind the nearest cluster of snow-covered pine trees.

Standing upright, they were about seven feet tall and weighed several hundred pounds.

"What *are* they?" Dani whispered in horror. "Please say polar bears."

"No," Isabelle whispered, staring at them, reading them. She shook her head. "They're not animals, exactly."

Archie gulped. "I-I think they're, uh, y-y-yetis."

"What?" Jake asked, turning to him.

"Abominable snowmen!" Archie cried.

The middle one threw back its head and let out a roar, its blunt fangs gleaming in the silver moonlight. It pounded its chest like an ape.

Then the beasts charged.

CHAPTER NINE
Oh, Christmas Tree!

Y*etis?*

After all the giants, ghosts, and gargoyles Jake had dealt with in the past, he did not know how anything could shock him anymore. But he screamed right along with his friends at the terrifying sight of three huge abominable snowmen racing toward them.

"Quick! Get back in the sleigh!" He shoved the girls ahead of him toward the vehicle.

"What about Humbug?" Dani exclaimed.

"Never mind him! Red, get us out of here!" he hollered.

Their quarrels from the Spiteful Spice forgotten, they ran as best they could through the deep snow, sinking with every step, pulling each other along. In the next moment, they were all scrambling into the sleigh.

Red let out a warning roar, as if to say, *Hurry up! They're coming!*

The angry yetis were bearing down on them, their long, powerful arms swinging, plumes of snow kicking up behind them as they bounded and loped along.

"Ew, they smell," Dani muttered, covering her nose.

But the creatures' sharp stink was the least of their worries.

Jake was more concerned about getting his arms ripped off. His hands shook a little as he freed the reins from their brass holder. "Take us up, Red, now!"

"We're not going to make it!" Archie shouted.

Jake feared he was right. Red had to get a running start to pull the sleigh up into the sky; with its sled-like runners instead of wheels, the vehicle wasn't made for sharp turns. That meant that Red had to run straight for several yards—much too close to the charging yetis.

His heart thudding, Jake saw the nearest one change course slightly, cutting off their path.

Before the sleigh could lift off the ground, the beast ran into position a few yards straight ahead of them, blocking their escape.

It pounded its chest with a roar, waiting for them, while the other two surged closer.

Red tried to veer off in another direction, but was mindful of the fact that if he turned too suddenly, the whole sleigh could tip over. Jake saw the situation.

"Just keep going straight, boy! I'll get this brute out of the way!" He brought up his hand, cleared his mind with a will, and then used his telekinesis to fling the beast aside.

The yeti let out a startled yelp as it flew out of their way. Red thundered on like a racehorse, and the kids held on tight as the sleigh floated up a few feet off the ground.

The four of them started to cheer, but it was too soon to declare victory—a fact they realized in the next moment, to their horror.

The sleigh had only just started to clear the beasts' height, rising eight or nine, maybe ten feet off the ground—when, suddenly, the largest yeti, a huge silverback with a chipped fang, ducked low on his next loping stride.

He pushed off with his knuckles and used the extra heave of force to jump high into the air, reaching for the sleigh.

Jake shot a bolt of telekinesis at the yeti, but at his awkward angle, with the beast coming up underneath, he missed.

The yeti grabbed hold of the sleigh's runner and pulled the whole thing down out of the air.

Red let out a vengeful eagle scream, yanked out of the sky, while the kids shrieked, tumbling out of the vehicle into the deep snow.

They each crashed through the frozen top layer and disappeared into the freezing cold drifts of white powder.

At least while they were buried the yetis could not find them for a moment.

Dazed by the fall, Jake heard a terrible crack of breaking wood as the angry silverback smashed the sleigh.

Red yelped, still attached to the ruined vehicle by the harness.

Oh no! The Gryphon would be a sitting duck out there, Jake thought. The realization brought him back from his daze, then a piercing scream sounded nearby.

He knew that voice at once.

Blast it, one of the beasts had reached down into the snow and caught the carrot-head.

Jake climbed to his feet, reaching for Risker, his magical runic dagger, sheathed at his side. Dani O'Dell might be the bane of his existence, but nobody messed with her.

"Put her down!" he bellowed at the towering beast.

Her fists were swinging and her legs were kicking furiously, but she could not reach the yeti with any of her blows. The yeti held the small girl up at arm's length, looking confused about what sort of ferocious little prey he had captured.

Jake clenched his jaw and brandished his knife, while Archie and Isabelle's heads popped up out of the snow nearby. He heard his cousins gasp to find Dani captured.

"Hold still, carrot, I don't want to hit you," Jake warned through gritted teeth.

She did.

Jake drew back and hurled his dagger at the yeti.

The runic blade bit deep into the beast's upper arm. The creature dropped Dani with a howl of pain.

Landing in the snow, she instantly scrambled toward them.

"Good aim, Jake," she said in a shaky voice.

"Thanks." He glared in the monster's direction as he pushed her behind him with the others. Meanwhile, Risker dislodged itself from the beast's arm and floated back toward its master.

As a gift from the Norse god, Odin—a reward to Jake for his deeds in Giant Land—the runic dagger had been forged by the same legendary smith of Asgard who had fashioned Thor's hammer. Like the sky god's famous weapon, the knife was made to fly back into the hand of its owner.

Jake caught it out of the air and wiped the yeti's blood off it on the snow. "Isabelle, are you sensing anything useful from these beasts?"

She shook her head with a dire look. "Nothing that would surprise you. We landed in their territory. They just want to kill us—and, er, probably eat us."

"Blimey," Archie muttered.

Jake nodded. "You lot, go take shelter under that big tree," he ordered, shoving both girls none too gently in the direction of the largest pine tree in a grove a few yards away. Its dense, needled branches went all the way down to the ground. "Get as close to the trunk as you can. The branches should make it harder for them to reach you."

"What are you going to do?" Archie countered.

"I've got to free Red from that harness before he breaks his wings." Jake nodded grimly toward their ruined vehicle.

The big silverback was fixated on it, slamming the broken sleigh back and forth. As a result, poor Red kept getting banged around violently. He could not escape, because he was strapped to the vehicle by the harness.

"Be careful," Isabelle said.

Jake nodded. "Go!"

They did, racing toward the shelter of the great pine tree. Jake knew they'd need a little time to climb through the tight lattice of sharp-needled branches.

But they hadn't even reached the tree yet when the first yeti—the one Jake had thrown aside with his telekinesis—homed in on the kids running toward the pine tree.

It let out a roar and started chasing them.

Jake scanned the landscape for any way to buy them a few precious seconds to reach safety. A dead spruce tree nearby caught his eye.

He concentrated hard, summoned up his powers, then used his telekinesis to knock the dead tree over. With a mighty creak, it crashed to earth, landing on the yeti.

Jake couldn't tell if the murderous beast was dead or just unconscious, but with it safely pinned under the trunk, he ran to save Red.

On the way, from the corner of his eye, he noticed a crimson trail of blood on the snow leading back toward the forest. It seemed the yeti he had cut with Risker had turned tail and run away.

That left only the big silverback to deal with, but Jake was not eager to confront the colossal, hairy beast. His main objective was merely to cut Red free of the leather harness that had trapped and entangled him.

Guilt filled him as he approached the Gryphon who had saved him so many times. The poor creature would be lucky if he didn't break his neck, getting thrown around like that. Jake wished he had never put Red in that harness or made him pull the sleigh.

All of this was his fault. Dani had been right about what she had said in the sleigh. He should have done this alone. Once again, he had dragged everybody into danger, all because he could not resist the thrill of a new adventure.

Selfish as ever. I hope you're happy now, he thought bitterly.

Then he put aside his self-recrimination, moving stealthily toward his battered pet lying in the snow.

Red's magical crimson feathers were strewn across the ground; his lion fur was caked with snow. Jake was terrified at the sight of the noble beast hurt and barely conscious.

He could not tell how badly the Gryphon was injured or if anything was broken—but it was plain the sleigh could not be used again.

It was only good for firewood at this point.

Which meant they were stranded out here.

He shook off a shudder of dread at the thought.

He could not let himself think about that right now, or he'd be paralyzed with fear. He had to act quickly.

The yeti was slamming the broken frame of the sleigh over his head, fixated on banging it against the snow-covered ground. Most of the chassis was caved in. The sled-like runners on the bottom were splintered.

One ski was ripped off entirely, the other broken into a sharp, spear-like point.

The yeti paused, looking over at Jake as he crouched down by Red's side. The huge creature's red eyes gleamed with a malevolent light, homing in on him.

"You stay back!" Jake swallowed hard, resting his hand on the Gryphon's furry shoulder. "Get up, boy. C'mon, Red. I'll cut you free. We got to get away from that thing. Can you stand up?"

A pitiful sound escaped his feathered friend, something like, *"Tweek."*

The yeti threw down the sleigh and stood up to its full, terrifying height. It let out a roar that made its intentions clear—and gave Jake a good look at its long ivory fangs.

Looming against the starlight, the reeking, matted beast stood well over seven feet tall, probably four feet wide at the shoulders.

It took a step toward him.

"Get back!" Jake yelled instinctively, even though he knew the brute animal could not understand him. He had no choice but to summon up his powers even though he was aware that using them again would weaken him. In this frozen landscape, he would need every ounce of his strength, but Red's life was at stake.

The yeti bent its hairy knees, gathering itself to spring. At the same time, Jake brought up his hands with the full force of his telekinesis and pushed the air toward the animal with all his might.

The giant yeti went flying backward.

It landed maybe thirty yards away in a snow drift, but in a heartbeat, Jake saw that he had only made it angry.

At once, he unsheathed Risker with a soft metallic zing. He reached for the first strap of the harness that held the Gryphon captive and sliced it in two.

The yeti exploded out of the snowdrift.

Jake could hear his friends screaming warnings from the direction of the pine tree, where they were concealed.

His hands were shaking as he stumbled a few steps away to cut the second strap of Red's harness.

The Gryphon was struggling to stand up when the yeti leaped at them, covering a shocking span of ground.

Jake gripped the second strap in one hand and fumbled with his knife—partly out of fear, partly because his hands were half frozen. He hesitated for half a heartbeat, wondering if he should wallop the yeti again with his telekinesis. His fleeting uncertainty cost him a sliver of a second that he could not afford.

The yeti's huge leap landed him next to the ruined sleigh; he picked it up again at once. Refusing to be separated from the helpless Gryphon, Jake had no time to do anything but hold on.

He dropped his dagger in the snow and, with both hands, grasped the strap still holding Red captive.

The enraged yeti lifted the sleigh over his head, then hurled it with a thunderous roar toward a grove of the large, snowy pine trees.

They went whipping through the air, Jake holding on to the long leather rein of the harness, shouting as he flew.

Red flapped his wings a few times frantically, trying to backpedal, but it was useless. In the next moment, both of them crashed into the boughs of the nearest pine tree.

Jake shut his eyes as he took a face full of the thick snow coating the branches, then he was falling, sharp needles scratching at his cheeks...

Chaos and darkness, blindly falling, slipping, scrabbling to catch himself; the sound of cracking wood all around him, groaning branches, sticky sap, piney smell. A pair of snowy owls flew out of the branches with scandalized squawks, and the yeti roared below.

At last, Jake stopped falling. He opened his eyes and found himself still stuck in the tree, high above the ground. But at least he was out of the monster's reach for the moment.

He shook his head to clear it and tried to get his bearings, still holding on to the strap for dear life.

Fortunately, there was a sturdy branch just beneath his feet, so he was able to step down and brace himself on it, though his legs were shaking. "Red?" he called anxiously.

The Gryphon dangled by his harness a yard or so above him, like some sort of giant Christmas tree ornament. "Becaw!"

Jake glanced down, wondering if yetis could climb trees. Probably so, he thought, ape-like as they were. But the yeti on the ground was not the only source of danger.

Peril came from above them, as well. The wreckage of the sleigh was precariously lodged in the branches over his head.

That thing's coming down, Jake thought, realizing they had to get away from that spot. More importantly, Red was still attached to the ruined sleigh. He had to cut him free.

They didn't have much time. But he'd left his knife below.

Finding a secure foothold in the massive pine tree's branches, Jake let go of the strap and climbed out of the sleigh's path, then reached out his hand. "Risker, come to me!"

From far below, a glint of silver on the snow was his runic dagger rising from the ground in answer to his call.

Jake's heart pounded as it floated slowly toward him.

It was certainly taking its time.

"Hurry up, you stupid knife!" he yelled as the yeti started shaking the tree. "Hold on, Red!"

The brute seemed to think it would be easier to shake them down rather than bothering to climb up after them.

The yeti proceeded to rock the massive pine tree at its base, trying to knock them off the branches like a couple of large, juicy pieces of fruit that it intended to eat as soon as they hit the ground.

As their furry tormentor put his shoulder into the task, the smell of wet, stinky yeti rose through the branches and filled Jake's nostrils.

The tree shook like it was caught in the gales of a hurricane.

Red swung back and forth from the harness, until he finally bared his lion claws and sank them deep into the wood of the branches around him, anchoring himself.

Meanwhile, the broken sleigh above them started inching out of its position.

"Risker, quickly!" Jake pleaded. As the tree swayed, the magic knife wound its way through the dense pine boughs.

Jake let go of his death grip on the trunk, reaching out to grasp the dagger's hilt. *There!* He had it at last. "Hold on, Red, I'm coming!"

Putting the knife between his teeth, pirate-like, he climbed up the violently swaying tree, desperate to reach the Gryphon and cut him loose before the sleigh fell back down to earth and took Red with it. This time, the Gryphon might not survive.

At last, Jake crawled into position near Red's side. Ignoring sharp needles poking him everywhere, he hooked his knee around one branch and braced himself with the other leg, as well. He had no choice but to let go with his hands in order to complete the task.

Then there came a rasping sound above him as the sleigh started to slide out of the shaking tree's branches. Jake gasped.

Pulse pounding, he grasped the strap in his left hand, took his knife in his right, and severed it with an awkward chop just as the sleigh plunged out of the branches overhead with a groan of creaking wood.

He ducked, cursing under his breath as the sleigh ripped past them, plummeting toward the ground.

The yeti stepped back to see what sort of progress he was making. Jake saw the beast's red eyes widen as the sleigh came crashing down on top of him.

It knocked the yeti flat on his back—and impaled him on the sleigh's broken runner.

Jake grimaced as the yeti's final, ferocious roar was cut short.

Then, silence.

What a relief.

Chest heaving, Jake looked over at the Gryphon.

"Becaw?" Red asked weakly.

"It's all right, boy," he panted in exhaustion. "He's dead."

No more yeti.

CHAPTER TEN
Stranded

The others came running while Jake climbed down the massive tree.

"Are you all right up there?" Dani yelled.

"More or less. Not sure about Red, though." He jumped off a lower branch onto the ground, his legs still a bit shaky after that ordeal.

Dani steadied him, then they both looked up in concern and watched the bruised and battered Gryphon circle down to join them with a few weary flaps of his scarlet wings.

When Red landed on the snow, Jake was finally able to inspect him. "How are you, boy? Anything broken?"

"Becaw." Red shook his head.

Jake gave him a pat. "Well, at least I got to rescue you for once, instead of the other way around, eh?"

Red nuzzled him like an oversized housecat to show his appreciation, nearly knocking him over. Jake chuckled.

Meanwhile, Archie and Isabelle were staring at the dead yeti with their mouths hanging open.

"Hideous!" the boy genius finally exclaimed.

The creature's face was frozen in a snarl, fangs bared. Jake winced at the sight of the stake driven through the dead yeti where the sleigh had landed on him.

But Dani marched over and gave the lifeless monster a vengeful kick in the side. "Serves you right! Why don't you pick on someone your own size next time?"

Archie raised his eyebrows at her, then pointed at the other unmoving yeti, still pinned under the fallen tree. "I'm not sure if that one's dead or unconscious, but either way, I don't think we should spend any more time here than absolutely necessary. There could be more of these abominables waiting in the woods for us."

"Agreed," Jake said. "We should be on our way."

"But how? What are we going to do?" Dani gestured at their smashed vehicle. "The sleigh's ruined. Red can't carry us all, especially in his condition."

The Gryphon took a couple of limping steps. "Caw!" he offered, as if to say, *I'll try.*

"No, Red, you can't. Look at you, poor thing! You were so brave." Dani hugged their feathered friend.

"Why don't you go take a rest under those trees where we were hiding, Red?" Isabelle suggested. "The low branches make it nice and sheltered from the wind. Lie down for a few minutes while we work out what we're going to do next."

"Good idea," Jake agreed, nodding. "We'll let you know as soon as we're ready to go."

The noble beast hesitated.

"Ah, go on, boy," Jake insisted. "We'll be fine here. That yeti could've killed you. You need to rest up and save your strength. There's no telling what we might have to face next."

"Caw." Red seemed to see the wisdom of this warning and accepted their suggestion. He flew off toward the stand of trees the others had left a few moments ago and crawled into their abandoned hiding place.

"All right, so what are we going to do?" Isabelle asked, propping her hands on her waist.

"Excellent question, sis. Hate to be a killjoy," Archie said, "but if we don't get to some sort of real shelter soon, we'll probably die of hypothermia within, oh, three hours at best, by my estimation."

"Three hours to live?" Dani cried.

"If it's any consolation, it's not a bad way to go," Archie said apologetically. "You'll get very cold and very tired, and then you just...fall asleep."

"Oh, that makes me feel so much better!" Dani said. "The yetis might as well have killed us, then! We're already doomed."

"No, we're not. Don't say that," Jake ordered.

"But it's true, isn't it?" Anger and fear gleamed in her green eyes. "Archie knows about such things. And look at us! We're stranded in the middle of nowhere. The sleigh's in splinters. We have no idea where we are and we're already half frozen."

All of that was true, and Jake already felt horrible about dragging them into this. Guilt, however, was not a helpful emotion when one had to rack one's brain for solutions.

Raking his hair out of his eyes, he turned away and strove to focus on the problem right in front of them. "Look," he said sternly after a moment. "Our only hope now is to catch that stupid elf again. He's the only one who knows his way around this snowy wasteland. At this point, I'm happy to forget about taking him back to Santa's for the reward, if he'll just show us how to get to the North Pole."

And let's hope Santa's compound isn't more than three hours away, he thought, though he did not say that part aloud. Everyone was already scared enough.

"Well, at least he won't be hard to follow." Archie pointed across the snowfield.

Jake and the girls looked, then they all smiled ruefully. At last, one thing had come out in their favor. The fleeing elf had left an obvious trail behind him—not footsteps in the snow, but something just as easy to follow. Humbug's escape tunnel had bumped up the snow above it, like when a mole digs under a nice, green stretch of summer lawn.

As a result, his escape route was plain.

Of course, there was no telling how far ahead of them the little miscreant had already traveled. Fast as he was, Humbug might be a mile or more ahead by now.

But at least this gave them a chance of finding him.

"Right!" Archie declared in as cheerful a tone as he could muster under the circumstances. He clapped his gloved hands together and rubbed them to keep warm. "Well, then, let's get on with it."

Isabelle sighed and shook her head. None of them were eager for this trek. "It'll be slow going in this deep snow."

"Too bad we don't have any snowshoes," Dani said.

"Hey, maybe I can make some," Archie said all of a sudden. "Quick, help me find my tool-bag. It was in the sleigh."

"You brought your tool-bag?" Dani asked.

"Don't you know by now he doesn't leave the house without it?" Jake jested, then he clapped his cousin on the back. "Good man! You always come through, Arch."

"Always be prepared," he answered with a modest grin.

Then they all started searching through the wreckage of the sleigh strewn about the area, until, at last, shivering, teeth chattering, they found Archie's tool-bag sinking in the snow.

The ever-resourceful boy genius got to work immediately fashioning snowshoes for them. He bent thin, flexible pine boughs into a tennis-racket shape, then strung them with long, tough hairs off the dead yeti.

Their luck further improved when Jake discovered a box of matches in the bottom of Archie's tool-bag. The sleigh was unusable for transportation, but they could always burn it for firewood.

Jake started tearing it apart and piling up the wood.

"Do you want some light?" Dani suddenly asked Archie. He was squinting to thread the snowshoes by nothing but moonlight. "We could get the carriage lanterns burning."

"A fine idea, Miss O'Dell," Jake interjected, tossing aside an armload of broken carriage planks. "They should still have oil in them. C'mon, carrot. Give me a hand."

While Archie hurried to finish his makeshift snowshoes, Isabelle trudged off to check on Red. Jake and Dani salvaged the carriage lanterns off the ruined sleigh. They lit one with a match and cheered as the feeble circle of light spread around them and began to glow, warding off the darkness of the arctic night. They agreed to save the second lamp for later, knowing the first would eventually run out of oil.

Perhaps we'll all be dead by then, Jake mused. Then he scolded himself for allowing such thoughts. Despair was an emotion unbefitting a future Lightrider.

Before long, they all had on their snowshoes and were ready to go. Jake gave the lantern to Isabelle and made torches for everyone else, lighting pieces of wood from the broken sleigh. Red seemed a bit better after a short rest. Now all that remained was to follow Humbug's tunnel trail until they caught up with the elf.

"Before we set out, uh, there's just one quick thing I wanted to say," Jake said.

They were standing around in a circle, making their final checks. Everyone glanced at him. The flickering torchlight revealed the uncertainty on all their faces, but so far, their courage held.

"What is it, Jake?" Isabelle prompted, although as an empath, no doubt, she already knew what he was feeling.

He looked around at them with a guilty pang, then lowered his head. "I'm just...really sorry I got you into this. I just wanted to have, you know, a Christmassy adventure. I never intended for anything like this to happen. I didn't even know yetis exist!" He shook his head in awkward frustration. "I-I just wanted to say that I'll do all in my power to make sure we get back safe. And, er, alive."

They gazed fondly at him, then laughed a bit and shook their heads, glancing around at one another.

"What?" he asked, a trifle defensively.

"No worries, old chap." Now it was Archie's turn to give him a jovial slap on the back. "I think I speak for all of us when I say we expected nothing less."

The girls nodded, chuckling as they walked away.

"We all know you love nearly getting us killed," Dani shot back over her shoulder, laughing.

Jake scowled after them, then followed.

* * *

Humbug's little tunnel seemed to stretch out ahead of them forever into the vast, white, arctic unknown.

Jake began to wonder if Archie's estimate of three hours before hypothermia set in had been overly optimistic.

They encouraged each other for as long as they could, but eventually, even words took too much effort as their faces went numb. The cold was as cruel and ruthless as a Dark Druid's obsidian blade. The snow kept coming, and as it blew in the wind, it threatened to hide the bump of Humbug's tunnel leading them on.

They gave up trying to hurry, as every step took more effort. It was awkward enough to walk in the makeshift snowshoes. Jake didn't care to wonder how much slower their progress would have been without them.

They kept their heads down, each silently praying for a miracle, while the frigid gusts snuffed out their torches one by one, until only the lantern burned.

Strangely enough, the weaker they got, the stronger Red seemed to become—though perhaps it was nothing more than fear that renewed his energy.

He was worried about the children, seeing them inch across the snow without talking at all, shuffling like half-frozen sleepwalkers. Their hair was coated in ice; snow caked their coats and clung to their eyebrows. Tiny ice crystals formed on their lashes, and he feared that at any moment now, Dani O'Dell in particular, the littlest of them, was going to fall down into the snow, unconscious.

How much farther?

They didn't have much time. The blowing winds sculpted the snow in shifting dunes. If it covered Humbug's tunnel, disguising the bump in the snow, then soon, they'd have nothing left to follow. They'd be well and truly lost.

Thinking ahead (for he was an unusually clever beast), the Gryphon gave a low caw to let his charges know he was flying aloft. To be honest, his wings were going numb. He did not know how much longer they would work in this cold.

He flapped up into the sky to see where the path led, how much farther the elf's tunnel went. The wind tossed him about, but he fought to stay on course, circling to see if he could spy any possible shelter for his children. If he had to, he would put them on his back one by one and fly them to safety—if any safe place could be found.

But then, he saw it in the distance—a light! A structure of some kind. Santa's compound? He couldn't be sure, but the elf's tunnel led straight to it.

With a loud, eager caw, Red flew back down and nudged Isabelle awake from where she had paused, just standing there with her eyes closed. *Wake up!*

"Becaw!"

"Huh?" She blinked herself back to awareness. "Oh...I must have drifted off. That's not good..." Then she noticed the others had done the same.

Jake was on his feet, though motionless, his eyes closed, in much the same state as she had been a moment ago. But, glancing around, she gasped in dread to find Dani and her little brother curled up on the ground, sleeping. Already the snow was blowing over them, starting to cover them forever. She rushed to get them on their feet. "Wake up! Jake, help me!"

She reached out and shook him by his shoulder, then pointed at the younger pair when he turned around with a groggy look of question.

He, too, gasped with horror when he saw them and instantly dropped to his knees to help her wake them up. "Hey!"

Jake slapped their faces lightly, bringing them back to awareness. "Come on, get up, you two! Dani! Archie! On your feet!" he yelled at them. "If we fall asleep out here, we'll die!"

"Caw, caw, becaw!"

"What is it, Red?" Isabelle turned and looked intently at the Gryphon, using her telepathic powers to read his thoughts. She drew in her breath at his news. "Really? How far?"

"Caw!" He bobbed his head toward the distant ridge.

"What is it?" Jake asked as he pulled Archie to his feet.

Archie blinked, trying to shake off sleep.

"Give me a hand," Jake muttered. Then both boys hauled the still-sleeping Dani upright.

"Red says there's a building ahead!" Isabelle reported. "He says we're almost there!"

"Santa's c-c-compound?" Archie chattered.

"He's not sure. Probably so. It's just beyond that ridge!" she answered, pointing to the north.

Red breathed on Dani to try to warm her up, and spread his wings to shelter them all from the wind for a moment until they were ready to continue.

Dani rubbed her eyes. "Sorry," she mumbled. "I can't believe I fell asleep. I'm *soooo* tired."

"We all are," Isabelle said, giving her a worried hug.

"Take hold of whatever strength you've got left," Jake encouraged them. "It's not much farther. Red says we're almost there."

"Really?" Dani asked wistfully.

"Let's all hold on to each other so no one falls asleep again," Isabelle suggested. "We don't want to lose anyone."

They linked arms, even though it made the slow going even slower. At least now there was no possibility of anyone falling behind.

Red walked a few steps ahead of them, leading the way, and keeping his wings spread to try to shield them from the wind.

"Maybe we should think of a game or something to help us keep going," Archie said slowly.

Dani groaned. "I don't feel like playing any game. My face is so cold I can hardly talk."

"Why don't we sing?" Isabelle said.

"No, thank you," Jake muttered.

"Count, then," Archie said. "Just count off numbers, one by one. That'll help us stay awake. Come on, you can count, can't you? Simple. Count the steps. One!" he sounded off.

"Two," said Isabelle.

"Three," Dani forced out.

"Four," Jake said.

"Caw!" Red chimed in.

"Six..."

Anyone who was too slow to say their number got an elbow from the person beside him or her.

"I can't wait until we get there. I wonder what Santa will be like. And Mrs. Claus. And the reindeer."

"I hope he gives us hot chocolate."

"Of course he will."

"I hope he has a blazing fire in the hearth."

"And a place to lie down."

"Do you think he'll help us get home?"

"He has to! We might have to wait until after Christmas, though. This is his busiest time of year," Archie pointed out.

"Mother and Father will be very cross if we're not home for Christmas," Isabelle said wearily.

"Aunt Ramona will be furious if we miss the Nativity pageant," Archie said. "She'll probably turn us all into newts."

"Nonsense. They'll all just be glad that we're alive." Jake's legs burned with every step as they climbed the frigid slope before them.

But when, at last, they arrived at the crest of the ridge and saw the building below, the hurrahs died on their lips.

It was not what they had expected.

Indeed, Jake felt his hopes shatter like brittle ice at the sight of the dark, foreboding castle.

A single, pale blue light shone in the tower like a cold, watchful eye.

Dani sent him a fearful glance, looking for reassurance, but he had none to give.

It looked deserted.

Isabelle shook her head in dismay. "I don't think that's Santa's compound."

"It certainly doesn't look very jolly," Dani agreed.

"But look! Humbug came this way. There's his trail." Archie pointed down the hill.

Sure enough, barely visible anymore in the shifting winds, the little bump-up in the snow led right up to the ominous castle gates.

The gates stood open, as though someone was expecting them, Jake thought uneasily. But no. They were probably just frozen into place like that.

He scanned the area, but saw no obvious signs of danger—nor any real signs of life. Maybe the castle *was* deserted except for the grumpy elf, who had apparently made a beeline for this place. Jake shook his head in grim uncertainty, but what else could they do?

"Come on, then," he said. "It's the only shelter available. Let's go."

"I don't have a good feeling about this, Jake," Isabelle murmured.

"Me neither. But if we stay out here, we're doomed."

They started down the slope. Catching each other when they stumbled in the deep snow, they followed Humbug's tunnel to the gates.

Jake noticed large boot prints on the ground. *Hmm.* Those looked recently made, and the feet that made those imprints were much too big for any Christmas elf.

Above them, the frozen pair of watchtowers that overlooked the gates were deserted. No soldiers on duty. *Where the devil are we? Whose castle is this?* he wondered, but he hid his growing fears as he led his companions up to the castle's icy front door.

He was tempted to just go in, but on second thought, that could be bad for their health.

Instead, he reached up and grasped the huge metal knocker, rapping the rusty ring loudly against the thick wooden door.

They waited, huddled together and chattering.

"There's nobody here," Dani said, sounding on the verge of crying.

"Can you sense anyone in there?" Archie asked his sister.

Isabelle shook her head. "Hard to say. It seems to be protected by magic."

"Caw!" Red urged him.

Jake nodded and took a step back. "I'll get us in there." He lifted his hands, praying he had enough strength left to use his telekinesis to blast the door open.

But before he could summon up his powers, suddenly, whether

by magic or by some unseen mechanism, the massive door swung open slowly with a loud, ominous creak.

Swirls of frost whirled around them, but when the door had banged open wide, nobody was there.

Ahead stood a vast, dark hall, full of drafts and echoes.

They exchanged nervous glances.

"Maybe Humbug opened the door for us," Dani whispered.

Jake shook his head. *I don't think so.* "Stay on your guard, everyone," he warned. Then he led the way, stepping over the threshold with the others right behind him.

CHAPTER ELEVEN
The Fortress of Frost

They had crept only a few stealthy steps into the castle when the door slammed shut behind them. Everyone jumped. Holding on to each other, they ventured on with Red right behind them.

There were no signs of life indoors, either, just echoes in the silence, and the howling of the wintry wind outside.

Pillars flanked the long, dark corridor before them.

"Is it just me, or do you feel like we're being watched?" Archie murmured.

Jake nodded.

"It looks like someone's waiting for us up ahead," Isabelle whispered, pointing.

A pale blue light like the one they had seen glowing in the tower flickered at the end of the stone corridor.

Dani gulped. "Maybe we should just stay here."

Jake knitted his brow with determination. "It's probably just that stupid elf. C'mon."

But the moment they stepped out of the narrow corridor into the wider space beyond, bright lights suddenly flashed all around them, blinding them after hours in the dark.

Worse, a terrible roar from nearby made everybody scream.

While the lights continued flashing, the roar was joined by a pair of bloodcurdling howls on either side of them. Clumped together in panicked confusion, the kids kept on screaming—all the more so when their eyes adjusted and showed them the enormous polar bear rearing up on its hind legs just a few feet in front of them.

A polar bear dressed in a blue satin waistcoat.

Huh? Jake thought, momentarily startled out of his terror. He glanced to the side. Likewise, the howls came from two large silver wolves standing guard at the end of the corridor.

The wolves wore plumed helmets on their heads.

And though all three animals bared their vicious fangs, none of them actually attacked.

"Silence!" a female voice commanded. "That will do."

At once, the bear and the wolves stopped making all the noise.

Still squinting against the bright light, Jake saw that they were standing in the great hall of an ice palace.

Ice flowers. Ice furniture. Even a mock fireplace with ice sculpted into flames instead of a real fire.

Above the ice-block mantel hung an oval portrait of a hideous old woman with blue skin, wild gray hair, and a wart on the end of her crooked nose.

But that was not who sat on the ice throne in the center of the room.

As the polar bear dropped back onto all fours and withdrew with the wolves to stand obediently by the wall, Jake stared at the beautiful but strange figure of the ice queen seated on her crystalline throne.

She wore a crown of spiky silver icicles, but what made her appearance especially unnerving was that her face was covered by an eerie white Venetian carnival mask.

The long sweep of her white gown sparkled like the snow. It had a high standing collar of frozen lace that wrapped around the back of her neck in a regal fashion.

"So! Here are our spies, as expected. It seems you were telling the truth after all, Humbug."

"I told you, Your Highness."

Jake hadn't even noticed the elf's presence until now.

He looked over and saw Humbug caught in the clutches of a giant nutcracker in the shape of a toy soldier. The thing must have been seven feet tall. It loomed in silence beside the queen's throne, its wooden face unchanging, its painted eyes just staring.

Similar giant toy soldiers painted with royal blue uniforms stood at attention here and there around the ice hall. The nutcracker must have been the captain of the palace guard, however, Jake thought. He was painted the most ornately, with a gold sash across his chest and a saber by his side.

Not even Humbug, fast as he was, had much chance of getting away from the ice queen's wooden army. The little elf dangled from the nutcracker's grasp, with his painted-on white gloves.

Jake wondered if this was the welcome the elf had expected when he had decided to come here. *What is this place, anyway?*

He still had no idea what was going on.

The masked queen rose and glided toward them on razor-sharp ice skates. "So, spies. My grandfather sent you to check up on me, did he? Do you have anything to say for yourselves? Or shall I have my men torture it out of you?"

Red growled while Archie and the girls whispered to each other: "What? What is she talking about?"

"We're not spies!" Jake told her.

"Aha! Exactly what I'd expect a spy to say," she countered. "How else do you explain your lurking around the castle, then?"

"Please, ma'am, we're lost. We haven't the foggiest idea where we are," Archie attempted, always the diplomatic one. "We're sorry if we trespassed on your territory. We didn't mean to. We just really need some shelter."

"What, too cold for you out there today?" she drawled.

Jake took a step forward, bristling with anger. Everything in him warned that they needed to get out of there, but the prospect of going back outside was worse. "Look here, ma'am. We are not spies," he told her firmly. "We are simply trying to reach the North Pole."

"So you claim. And quit calling me ma'am. I'm not much older than you!" To their surprise, she whipped off her smooth, eerie carnival mask to reveal the face of a girl barely older than Isabelle.

Jake blinked, taken off guard by this revelation, and slightly confused for a moment about why the girl had been trying to seem so much scarier than she actually was.

He shook his head to clear it. "Look, whoever you are. I don't know what that elf might have told you about us, but we are not spies—and he is not to be trusted! He's a liar and a cheat. He nearly got us killed by yetis earlier tonight, simply as a distraction so he could escape."

"Escape?" she echoed. She skated closer. "Ah, then you admit you were holding him prisoner?"

"So what if we were?" Jake retorted. "That elf's got a bounty on his head. We're returning him to Santa to collect the reward."

"All lies!" Humbug cried, his little feet flailing as the nutcracker man held him fast. "They're Santa's agents sent here to spy on you, Your Highness! When I saw them lurking around the castle, I came here as fast as I could to warn you and your brother that you were once more under surveillance."

The girl scoffed. "As if they'd dare send spies out on my brother. No, Humbug, you've worked for my family long enough to know my grandparents would never subject the prince to their nonsense. Precious Jackie-boy can do whatever he wants. It's only *me* they bother with their constant rules and regulations—which is why I am never going back there!" She folded her arms over her chest.

"What prince? Who are you? What is this place?" Jake demanded.

"I'll ask the questions here!" she warned him. "And believe me, I have plenty of them. But first, we come to the basic problem: Humbug says you're spies, while you claim he's a fugitive. So it's your word against his, and frankly, I'm not sure I believe either one of you."

"But Your Highness, I told you they would come!" the elf protested. "The spies were chasing me and now, here they are, just like I said! Please, dearest Snow Maiden, you know me."

"I know you to be a bit of a rascal, Humbug," she admitted.

"Please, Miss," Dani spoke up in exhaustion, "do we really look like spies to you?"

The Snow Maiden stared at her, then looked at each of them in turn. "Well, if you are spies, you're not very frightening, actually. Except maybe him." She nodded dubiously at the Gryphon.

"Excuse me, but we just defeated three yetis out there," Jake informed her, rather insulted by the remark. "Maybe we don't seem like much at the moment, but that's because we're half frozen to death. Honestly! If you had any sort of decency, you'd offer us food and shelter. A fire to warm us? A place to rest would be nice! But if this is how you're going to be, whoever you are, then we'll take that lying elf off your hands and be on our way. Our business is with him and Santa Claus, not you."

"Now, now, don't be so touchy!" she exclaimed. "There's no need to go dashing off in a huff. This is my castle—"

"Er, actually, it belongs to your brother, Snow Maiden," Humbug pointed out.

Which earned him her glare.

"The point is, none of you are going *anywhere* until I am satisfied about who's telling the truth here. However," she conceded with a haughty lift of her chin, "I suppose there is something we can do about your other requests, if you're going to whine about it. We may be a thousand miles from civilization, but we are not devoid of hospitality here in the arctic circle. Guards!" she bellowed. "Show them to the guestrooms."

"How very kind," Isabelle offered at once, trying to smooth things over.

"But separate them," Snow Maiden ordered the giant toy soldiers. "If they *are* spies, let's not give them a chance to talk amongst themselves and coordinate their lies."

The toy soldier bowed, then beckoned stiffly with his wooden arm and started goose-stepping ahead of them toward the castle stairs.

She gestured to them to follow. "My servants will attend you," she said.

"Thank you," Jake said, feeling rather smug. He sketched a gentlemanly bow and Archie did the same; the girls curtsied.

The Snow Maiden smirked but stared after Jake as he led his friends out of the ice hall. "Perhaps you will be in a more pleasant mood after a meal and some rest. I do hope you come back prepared to explain yourselves. If not, there's always the dungeon."

The kids exchanged grim glances, still unsure if they were prisoners or guests in this strange place.

Then they and Red followed the giant toy soldier toward the castle's main staircase. A second soldier followed after them, making sure nobody strayed.

Jake wondered how the tall wooden figures managed to stay upright on the staircase with their long, awkward steps. The stairs were slippery as well, crusted with a thin coat of ice.

Archie came over to Jake and leaned toward his ear. "Who the blazes is she?" he whispered.

Still irked at the girl, Jake shook his head. "Don't know, don't care, as long as she gives us some food and a warm fire. But I imagine we'll find out soon enough."

After they picked their way up the treacherous icy staircase, the toy soldiers marched them down the upstairs hallway.

The guard ahead of them opened the first door and waited for one of them to go in.

"Well? Who's it going to be?" Archie murmured.

They glanced around anxiously at each other.

Being separated was the one thing none of them had counted on. It was so much easier to stay confident and figure out solutions when at least they had each other.

Dani looked up at the toy soldiers. "Can't we please share a guestroom? You must have one with two large beds. One for the boys, one for us."

The towering toy soldier's painted eyes stared blankly. His big, round, smooth head rotated back and forth.

"At least let the girls stay together, with Red to protect them," Jake insisted.

Denied. The toy soldier merely pointed to the chamber again.

Jake fumed. Not much for conversation, these blokes.

"Well, you're going to have to wait while I at least make sure the room is safe for my friends." He stepped past the guard into the room to see if it held any kind of threats against whichever one of them ended up staying in here. He did not trust that daft ice girl downstairs for one minute, especially after she had mentioned torture.

While the soldier goose-stepped over to the fireplace, took the brass kerosene lighter off the mantel by its long handle, and used it to start a fire in the hearth, Jake scanned the room in suspicion.

He threw open the closet and even checked under the bed before he was satisfied.

He returned to the hallway, where Isabelle wore a look of concentration, her eyes closed. Jake realized she was using her gifts to try to sense any unseen threats inside the castle.

"Anything?" Jake asked as he joined her.

She opened her eyes and then shrugged. "Not from them." She glanced discreetly at the toy soldiers. "They're only following the Snow Maiden's orders."

"Who is she?" Jake whispered. "And who are her grandparents? She sure seems angry at them. She mentioned a brother, too. Jack, right? A prince of some sort, and she must be a princess. Humbug did call the girl 'Your Highness.' Any idea who these people are?"

The others shook their heads.

"Why did she think we were spies?" Dani whispered.

"Obviously, Humbug lied about us," Jake answered in a low tone. "That must be why he was so keen to get here before us. I'll bet he thought that if he beat us here, he could manipulate the situation and use her to get rid of us for once and for all. Then he could continue on his merry way to Halloween Town. But I daresay his little scheme hasn't quite gone to plan, because she doesn't seem inclined to let him or any of us leave."

"Well, I've never heard of anyone called Snow Maiden," Isabelle said discreetly. "But I can tell you she has very strong emotions. I can sense them all the way from here. Temperamental and rebellious, definitely spoiled. But I don't sense that she's evil. If we treat her carefully, I believe we *should* be all right."

"Well, that's reassuring," Jake drawled. "What does she want from us?"

"I'm not sure she knows herself. All I can glean from her emotions is that she's very lonely and extremely bored."

"Great," Jake muttered.

"Can't say I blame her for that," Archie said. "Living out here in a snowy wasteland, nothing but oversized toys and a few animals to talk to. Anyone could go slightly batty under such conditions."

"Hmm." Jake absorbed this skeptically.

"Well, if she's going to give us food and shelter, we might as well accept it," Dani said. "It's better than freezing to death. And whoever she is, she can't be worse than the yetis."

"True," Jake said.

"Right, then." Archie stepped toward the doorway. "I'll take this room," he bravely volunteered. "Courage, all."

"See you soon, I hope," his sister said.

"Goodnight, Arch," Jake said grimly.

Dani gave him a small wave. "Bye."

Archie nodded goodnight to them, then the toy soldiers locked him in, ignoring Red's low growl of protest.

One by one, each of them in turn was locked up in a comfortable guest chamber, with a fire to bring life back into their bones. Jake saw the girls safely into their rooms. The Gryphon took the next chamber. Jake went last, using the extra time in the hallway to scope out any possible escape route. He had a feeling they might need one in the future.

Unfortunately, he saw none—but he did witness a strange scene when the toy soldiers marched him across an upper balcony to his room.

The balcony overlooked the great hall, where the Snow Maiden was still toying with Humbug.

She beckoned to the nutcracker. "Bring him to me. Now then, Humbug. What are we going to do with you?"

"Let me go on my way to Halloween Town?" the elf suggested.

She laughed with crystalline gaiety. "Oh, I don't think so! You don't really want to work for that nasty old Jack O'Lantern fellow. You're not cut out for that at all."

"Yes, I am!"

"Nonsense. You're not nearly terrifying enough. Have you ever even *been* to Halloween Town?"

"Once," Humbug said. "I peeked in. Well, it might take some getting used to, but I know I will fit in there."

She started laughing at him. "You're such an amusing little fellow! I still don't trust you, but you do make me laugh. And, after all, you were telling the truth about this much, at least: there *were* people following you, and they came here, just as you predicted. So, for that, and for your good intentions, trying to warn me about Santa's spies, you deserve to be rewarded. How it would irritate my grandfather if I managed to turn one of his elves into my own servant. I know! I'll make you my jester!"

"Your Highness, please, I want to be a goblin!" Humbug protested, but it was too late.

She tapped him with her icicle wand and a silver cloud of sparkling magic snow engulfed the elf.

When the whirling puff of magic cleared away, Humbug's appearance was transformed.

His green coat had turned white. His little breeches were pale silver, and instead of a pointy Christmas elf hat, he now wore a blue and silver jester's cap with jingle bells on its several points.

He saw himself in the reflection of an icy mirror across from the Snow Maiden's throne and looked appalled at his makeover.

The Snow Maiden clapped her hands in delight. "Much better! Now you're a proper jester. Go on, make me laugh."

The grumpy elf just stared at her, at a loss.

Jake raised an eyebrow as he watched.

Poor Humbug seemed to be asking himself in that moment if

running away from Santa had been the best idea.

The Maiden's pretty face took on a glower. She folded her arms across her chest. "I said, make me laugh."

"Oh dear." Humbug sighed.

Jake's humor at the little trickster's expense was short-lived, however. The toy soldier prodded him in the back with the blunt end of his lance, shoving him into the guestroom.

"Watch it!" he shot back, whirling around after he caught himself from stumbling.

The tall, blank-eyed soldier slammed the door in his face.

Jake heard it lock and forced himself to check his temper. *Blast it, what are we going to do?*

He had a bad feeling about this place, but even if they could escape, only darkness, subzero temperatures, and bloodthirsty yetis awaited them outside. Without Humbug, they still did not know the way to Santa's. There was no help for it.

They were stuck for now.

Captives of the ice princess.

CHAPTER TWELVE
Chilling with the Ice Princess

Butlers and waiters across the civilized world wore black and white tuxedoes as their uniform; therefore, the children were only marginally surprised when the Snow Maiden's servants turned out to be funny little penguins.

Jake could not imagine who had trained them, but they were surprisingly efficient, carrying in his meal on silver trays, skating around easily on their little yellow feet when it came time to clear away the dishes.

Better still, Isabelle was able to communicate with them, thanks to her telepathic gifts, which worked especially well on animals. She reported everything the penguins had told her when they were reunited three hours later, summoned from their rooms for an audience with the bored Snow Maiden.

"You're not going to believe this," Isabelle whispered as they gathered at the top of the slippery castle stairs, still groggy from their naps. "She's Santa Claus's granddaughter."

"What?" they exclaimed in hushed tones.

"Santa and Mrs. Claus have a granddaughter?"

"And a grandson!" Isabelle nodded emphatically. "Jack Frost! That's the prince Humbug mentioned. This is *his* castle!"

"You have got to be joking," Jake said.

But Dani started laughing in delight.

Archie furrowed his brow. "No wonder that girl's so spoiled, then. Santa's granddaughter? She probably got everything she ever asked for, year round."

"Until lately," Isabelle said, beckoning them closer. "Turns out Snow Maiden always helped her Grandfather Frost deliver toys, especially across Russia and Eastern Europe. She's very famous in those parts."

"Gigantic country, Russia," Archie mused aloud. "A lot of ground to cover. I should think Santa could use a little help there."

"Right, and she was always happy to help him deliver toys when she was little," Isabelle said. "But according to the penguins, now that she's growing up, she wants no part of Christmas anymore."

"Santa's own granddaughter doesn't like Christmas?" Dani exclaimed.

Isabelle shrugged. "I'm not sure exactly what the penguins meant by this, but they said that these days, the Snow Maiden's too cool for Christmas."

"Too cool...?" Archie echoed with a look of confusion. "As in temperature?"

"I don't know. Apparently that's some sort of slang term in the local dialect or something."

"Hmm." Archie tilted his head. "One of my anthropologist friends in the Royal Society once told me that Eskimos, or should I say the Inuit people, who live in these latitudes, have fifty words for snow. Maybe this 'cool' comes from them. But who knows?"

Dani shook her head. "I'm still in shock to hear that Santa's own granddaughter doesn't like Christmas."

"The penguins said she's bored of it, and jealous of all the care and attention Santa gives to everybody else when Christmas comes," Isabelle reported. "She's been undermining him a lot in recent years, but the penguins said the last straw came earlier this autumn, when the Snow Maiden switched a bunch of names between the Nice and Naughty lists just for fun."

Jake chortled. "Nice prank."

"Santa didn't think so, with Christmas right around the corner. They got into a great family row."

"Well, the holidays can have that effect on families," Archie said. "It's a shame."

"Anyway, she stormed out—she lived with her grandparents, from what I understand. But she told them she was leaving to start her *own* winter holiday with no Christmas trappings, no carols, no Christmas trees, no nothing."

"That's absurd," Archie said.

Dani was appalled. "No Christmas?"

Isabelle nodded. "She threatened poor Santa and Mrs. Claus that one day, the whole world would forget that Christmas had ever existed. Then she left Santa's compound and invited herself here to stay in a guest wing of her brother's castle."

"No wonder Humbug ran straight to her," Jake said. "They sound like kindred souls. He also decided he hates Christmas and ran away from Santa."

"Erase Christmas?" Dani shook her head, still trying to absorb the Snow Maiden's unthinkable proposal. "But it's Baby Jesus' birthday!"

"Look, our main concern right now is getting out of here," Jake reminded them. "What about Jack Frost? Did the penguins tell you anything about him? Maybe he's more reasonable than his sister."

"Er, no, sorry," Isabelle said dryly. "According to the penguins, Santa's grandson and heir apparent is a bit of a rowdy hellion. He's eighteen. He hasn't been home in days. The penguins said the last they heard, he was having a skiing party on top of the Matterhorn with some of the Valkyries."

"Valkyries?" Jake and Archie burst out in unison.

The boys glanced meaningfully at each other.

"Let's hope he doesn't make them angry," Archie muttered after a moment.

"You mean like we did?" Jake answered wryly.

After their recent visit to the land of Norse giants and Viking legends, the boys still couldn't decide if the dazzling beauty of the tall, gorgeous warrior women outweighed the horror of the hag form the Valkyries could take when they decided to turn nasty.

Just then, the silvery jingling of little bells heralded the arrival of Humbug at the bottom of the stairs in his new jester hat.

"Would you stop dawdling? Get down here!" he demanded. "Her Highness is waiting! And she doesn't like to wait."

Jake glanced at his companions, who were staring at the elf in astonishment. They had not yet seen Humbug's transformation.

The little fellow looked more annoyed at the world than ever. "Hurry up."

"Why does he look like that?" Dani whispered.

"I forgot to tell you, Snow Maiden's keeping him. She's not letting him go on to Halloween Town." He shrugged. "I guess she wanted him to match her décor."

"She'd better not try something like that on us," Archie mumbled.

"Come on. We'd better go before she sends those creepy toy soldiers up to fetch us," Dani said.

"Follow my lead when we meet with her," Isabelle advised. "We're the closest in age. I'll try to make friends with her, girl to girl."

"Be my guest," Jake said under his breath.

The ice-slicked stairs were too dangerous to walk down, but someone had already thought of that and had had the good sense to have an ice slide built right next to them.

The kids whizzed down it one by one, while Red flew down to the lower level. Humbug watched and waited below, looking annoyed as ever.

Then the little jester-elf led the way back to the great hall, his bells jangling. "Your guests, Maiden," he announced them in a grumpy tone as they rejoined their captor.

She turned with a swirl of snowflakes flying from her long white skirts. Jake was glad she had not put her eerie white mask back on. For some reason, it unnerved him.

"There you all are. Finally!" She skated closer. "I trust you enjoyed your rooms. Feeling better? Good," she said, indifferent to the answer.

Cold-hearted, thought Jake.

"Now then. First things first—and you had better tell me the truth. Are you spies or aren't you?"

"No," they said in unison.

"Excellent! I have decided to believe you. If you're lying to me, you'll be sorry. But provided you're telling the truth, now we can get down to the main reason you're here."

"What's that?" Isabelle asked in the friendliest possible tone.

"To have fun, of course!" the Snow Maiden exclaimed, clapping eagerly, much to their surprise. "My brother's not the only one who can have friends, after all. My blood is as royal as his own. Every princess needs an entourage."

"Entourage?" Archie echoed.

"But you don't do me any credit in those clothes," she declared, shaking her head with a frown. "Let's see if we can make some improvements here."

"Oh, no..." After what he'd seen her do to Humbug, Jake started backing away.

"W-what do you mean?" Isabelle asked.

She flashed an oh-so-sophisticated smile. "I'm going to make you all look *cool*."

Before anyone could protest, she tapped them all with her snowflake wand, one by one, in quick succession.

Just as had occurred with Humbug, they were each engulfed in a chilly little whirlwind of magic snow.

It was dizzying, rather like being inside a snow globe when somebody was shaking it. When the puff of magic cleared, they looked around at each other in shock.

Humbug stifled a laugh.

But the Snow Maiden folded her arms across her chest and nodded proudly. "Oh, that's good. Take a look." She nodded toward the ice mirrors all around the hall.

They stared at themselves in disbelief.

"I have purple hair!" Dani shouted when she finally found her voice.

Snow Maiden clapped her hands. "I know! You look adorable!"

Dressed in a puffy white satin coat that ended at her waist, a short lavender skirt, and thick white stockings, with ice skates on her feet, Dani turned away from the mirror with a look on her face like she very well might cry—until she saw Jake.

Who looked just as silly, if not worse.

Snow Maiden had dressed him up like some sort of Prince Charming ponce in a white military coat with gold epaulets and a shiny black belt. He had dark blue breeches on and black leather riding boots. Thankfully, she had not put ice skates on him, or he'd have already gone sprawling face first on the floor.

He supposed he should be grateful for that, but he could not get over what she had done to his hair. She had put some sort of frosty white freeze on it so that the longish blond forelock that usually hung over his eye had been lifted in a swooping wave that curled out from his forehead like a ski jump.

He looked perfectly bizarre, but then, the Snow Maiden seemed to *like* bizarre.

She was terribly fashionable.

Hand on hip, she turned to Isabelle. "Now you look like a friend who's cool enough for me. What is your name?"

"Isabelle...Bradford," she mumbled, unable to tear her shocked gaze off her own reflection.

Snow Maiden thought this over. "Hmm, you'll need a new name, as my right-hand person in my entourage. Henceforth, you will be known as Ice-a-belle. Much cooler."

Izzy's golden ringlets had gone magically into a complicated, upswept hairdo of the sort that only older girls back home were allowed to wear.

Her long, sparkly gown was an understated pink shade, with long, tight sleeves. But she was appalled at how the front of her princess-like overskirts were split to allow her to skate freely.

Instead of a ruffled petticoat underneath, she had only been given pink woolen leggings like Dani's white ones.

Isabelle was mortified. Back home, no one ever even *glimpsed* the outline of a respectable female's leg, other than when young ladies wore bicycle bloomers, which were considered very shocking.

The only other exception was with the sort of costumes worn by female performers in the circus—acrobats, tightrope walkers, and such. A gentleman's daughter simply did not *wear* such things, but Snow Maiden either didn't know or didn't care.

Or, as Jake suspected, she just liked being shocking for its own sake.

She was beaming with pride at her creation. "Well, Ice-a-belle, what do you think? How smart you look! It's very avant-garde."

"I feel indecent!" She tried to hold her split skirts back together, no doubt dreading to think what her governess would say.

"Don't worry, you can't see anything," her brother assured her with a sympathetic frown.

"And look at this clever young fellow! Ice-a-belle, who is this?" Snow Maiden asked.

"My brother, Archie," she managed, still red-faced with embarrassment.

"How did you do that?" Archie asked Her Highness.

"By magic, of course. We Clauses have elven blood."

"I see."

Snow Maiden had put the boy genius in gray wool trousers, a warm blazer of dark purple corduroy, a silver scarf, and a gray waistcoat covered in white snowflakes. Actually, Archie didn't look half bad. Except for his dark hair, which stuck up in all directions in frosted spikes, as though he had just given himself a mild electric shock with one of his scientific experiments.

Even Red had not escaped the Snow Maiden's passion for giving people high-fashion makeovers. The Gryphon wore a royal blue waistcoat like the one on her polar bear; the lordly yellow ascot around his neck brought out the gold in his beak.

Cunning as she was, the Snow Maiden had also encrusted his wings with a thin layer of ice so he could not fly away.

"Becaw," Red complained to Jake.

Who couldn't agree more.

"Look here, Princess." He turned indignantly to their captor. "I don't know what you think you're doing, but I demand you put us back to the way we were and let us go on our way."

"Oh, you demand?" she echoed. "Sorry, did you think you were in charge here? How funny! What is your name?"

"I am Jake Everton, the Earl of Griffon. This is my Gryphon, Red, who goes with my title."

"Cool." Nodding, she looked him over in the most embarrassing fashion, from his feet up to his head, inspecting her handiwork. "Trust me, this is a big improvement. For one thing, these clothes have a magic spell on them that will help to keep you warm. Secondly, you look good. I'd almost call you a handsome boy."

Jake was instantly flustered—enough to forget his demands for a second.

She laughed at him. "How old are you?"

"Twelve," he answered warily.

"Ew." The Snow Maiden grimaced.

"What's wrong with being twelve?" he retorted as his cheeks turned even redder.

"Well, you're much too young to be my beau. After all, I am sixteen," she announced with a worldly air.

Jake scowled, the words on the tip of his tongue: *Who ever said I want to be your stupid beau?*

He wanted a girlfriend like he wanted a hole in his head.

But then he saw Ice-a-belle send him a warning look from behind Santa's mad granddaughter and somehow he kept his mouth shut.

If Her Highness could do *this* to them in a good humor, he did not want to find out what she might do to them if she felt insulted.

She waved off her fleeting interest in him and turned away. "At least you're as tall as me. Therefore, you will be my dancing partner at the ball tonight."

"What ball?" Archie asked, slightly put out to find himself ignored, as usual, by a pretty girl.

Jake envied him, for this one was entirely spoiled and possibly demented.

"Oh, yes, entourage!" the Snow Maiden announced, beaming at them all. "We are going to have a *great* party tonight. Why should my brother be the one to have all the fun?"

Jake feigned ignorance. "Your brother?"

"Jack Frost." Snow Maiden rolled her eyes. "He's *such* an idiot. He's so irresponsible. He cannot even follow a schedule, you know. Half the time he sleeps in and forgets to end a blizzard he started a week ago. But just because he's a boy, Grandfather let him build this castle for his bachelor lodgings. He moved in here when he was my age. But can I have a place of my own? No, no, no, of course not. Because I'm a *girl*."

"Maybe your grandparents just wanted to get him out of the house," Dani piped up. Now that she had recovered from the shock of having purple hair, she set about trying to help Isabelle with their goal of getting on their captor's good side. "I have older brothers, too, and they can be horrid to live with. They eat everything in sight and their feet stink."

"Right you are! La, you are so cute, my little snowflake." Snow Maiden put her arm fondly around the purple-haired eleven-year-old. "Anyway, as you can see, the prince isn't here. If Jack were at home, you'd see the blue snowflake light shining in the tower. He's gone off with his friends again." She heaved a sigh. "They never let me come along. I've had the whole castle to myself for days. It's *so* dull. No wonder I'm bored silly. So let's have some fun! What shall we do first?"

"Ahem, as much as we'd like to stay, Your Highness, I'm afraid we really must be on our way," Jake said as tactfully as possible.

"Nonsense! You're going to love being here with me."

"No, really," Jake insisted. "We must be on our way. We have to take Humbug back to Santa, and then get home to England to spend Christmas with our kin. They're expecting us, y'see."

"And we've agreed to be in the Christmas pageant back in our home village of Gryphondale. They're counting on us," Archie added with an earnest nod.

Snow Maiden's eyes narrowed. "That is not my problem," she said crisply. "Now then. How shall we amuse ourselves today?"

"Caw," Red muttered.

Even the Gryphon could see they were getting nowhere.

"Er, what would *you* like to do, Your Highness?" Ice-a-belle asked politely.

"I know! What do you say to a few rounds of indoor bowling?"

Jake rolled his eyes, especially when this suggestion seemed to make Dani forget about the gravity of their situation.

Genuinely enthused, the purple-haired girl clapped her pink-mittened hands; she couldn't seem to help herself. "I love bowling!"

Snow Maiden grabbed her hand. "Then come with me! Come along, all of you!"

Isabelle forced a smile and Archie nodded reluctantly, but Jake rolled his eyes as the Snow Maiden sailed off ahead of them, skating down another icy hallway.

How ridiculous to spend the day bowling in one of the castle's sprawling, gilded, frozen staterooms, when he had serious business that needed to be handled!

Jake was beyond annoyed.

But then, who could resist a few games of bowls on a wintry day? Especially when they bowled with large snowballs, knocking over nervous penguins that Her Highness ordered into formation to serve as bowling pins.

"Just try to be patient," Isabelle whispered to Jake while Archie took his turn, Dani and the Snow Maiden watching him, all smiles.

Jake growled. "I suppose if we keep her entertained throughout the day, eventually we'll find our moment to escape."

"We'd better be careful, Jake. She's really desperate for some company. I wouldn't put it past her to hurt us if she interprets our escape as us rejecting her. She's not as tough as she's trying to seem."

He nodded in agreement. "Well, I'll tell you one thing. I don't fancy going up against that polar bear. Or those wolves. Or those creepy toy soldiers."

"What about Humbug? We still don't know where we're going without him to show us the way," Isabelle whispered.

They glanced over and saw the grumpy elf looking absolutely miserable in his new post as jester to the Snow Maiden. Every time she ordered him to tell a joke or make her laugh, he looked like he wanted to throw himself off a bridge.

"I think that little miscreant is as eager to get out of here as we are. At this point, I'm ready to make a deal with him," Jake said. "Who cares if he wants to go and work in Halloween Town? I won't stop him anymore, if he'll work together with us, so we can all get out of here."

"You'll give up on collecting the reward?"

"Gladly, if he'll just show us the way to Santa's. Once we get there, we can ask for help and eventually get home. I mean, Santa's sure to help us, don't you think?"

She nodded. "But you're right. For now, we just need to bide our time."

Then it was Jake's turn to bowl.

He picked up a waiting snowball about the size of a snowman's head and sent the nervous penguins an apologetic look. Down the lane, they squeezed their eyes shut, but braced themselves and held their ground as the ball came rolling at them.

A moment later, they scattered in all directions with a chorus of harried squawks.

"Strike!" Dani cheered.

CHAPTER THIRTEEN
Yule Be Sorry

A nother couple of hours passed. Jake wasn't sure what time it was because the night lasted twenty-four hours in the Arctic at this time of year. Considering they had left London in the evening, he could only guess that it had to be very late at night.

The four of them kept yawning, which their hostess did not appreciate, determined as she was—almost to the point of mania—to be entertained.

She discussed fashion with Isabelle and magically switched her own outfit ten times with a snap of her cold fingers. "Look at this, look at this, look at this..."

Each costume was more bizarre than the next.

When Ice-a-belle finally protested in the most polite tone possible that she really didn't follow fashion all that much, Snow Maiden abandoned her with a peevish scowl and turned to Jake to amuse her.

She snapped herself one last time into a sporty costume and then showed him how to play hockey, continually thwacking the puck into the frozen fireplace.

It got boring fast. Perhaps she didn't realize that as an aspiring Lightrider, a righter of wrongs and doer of great deeds, Jake was a rather more serious boy than one who simply devoted himself to games.

When he looked at her and heaved a sigh before whacking the puck yet again with the stick, she got the message and moved on, dragging Archie into a game of giant ice chess.

The slippery ice chessboard took up a whole room, and the chess pieces were beautiful waist-high ice sculptures—king, queen, bishop, knight, rook, pawn. Though the sculptures were heavy, they slid easily enough to whichever square the player chose.

Alas, the Snow Maiden grew dangerously annoyed when the boy genius failed to let her win.

Watching her, Jake mused that Santa's granddaughter must have somehow concluded that other people were merely toys, too, and only existed to amuse her.

After ice chess, she taught Dani some fancy ice-skating moves. This seemed to thaw the Maiden a bit; the carrot-head had that effect on people, in Jake's experience.

But when Dani asked her what it was like to go out delivering toys with Santa Claus, the chill returned to the Snow Maiden's pretty face. "I don't see why everybody thinks he's so great. He's pretty stupid, if you ask me."

They were scandalized by such words.

"Santa? Stupid?" Dani said.

Archie's jaw dropped with indignation.

Even Jake was startled by this claim.

"Why do you say that?" he asked.

She huffed. "Half the world doesn't even believe he exists, and he refuses to prove it to them," she said, then she braced her fists on her waist and imitated her jolly, fat grandsire: "'If they don't want to believe in me, they don't have to, dear. It's their choice. I'm hardly going to force them.'"

She dropped the act with a cold scoff. "He's such a fool. People don't deserve all his gifts, yet he goes on, year after year, wasting all his time on them. Do you know he spends 365 days a year thinking of good things that he can give to all those useless people out there, and hardly anybody even says thank you?"

She shook her head and looked away. "They're not worth it. But when I tried to tell him so—for his own good!—he shouted so loud at me, it cracked the ice for half a mile."

"It did?" Dani breathed.

She nodded. "He told me that if that's the way I feel about humanity, then I'm no grandchild of his, and I could go live with the Blue Hag."

"Who's that?" Jake asked.

"My old aunt, the Winter Witch." Snow Maiden pointed to the portrait of the hideous old woman above the fireplace. "I swear, she's the only person in the world who really understands me. Jack says I take after her. He doesn't mean it as a compliment, but that's the way I take it. She's very powerful and everyone's afraid of her."

"So, why didn't you go and live with her if you're so close? Why come here instead?" Jake asked.

She shrugged and twirled away, spinning briefly on her skates. "Oh, I don't know."

"Sure, you do," he persisted.

"Well, you know...there's a dark side of winter. Not Christmastime, that's all bright and jolly and annoying, but past then. When it's gray and dark and endless and it drags on month after month, and you feel like you haven't seen the sun in an age. The bleakness makes you heavy and haggard and brings on a peculiar despair. That's the part of winter that belongs to the Blue Hag. My brother Jack may be a reckless dunce, but at least he's fun. That's why I came here." She turned away and lowered her head with a moody look, as though feeling awkward after her very personal admissions. "Excuse me, I have to go send out the invitations for my party."

"Do you want any help?" Isabelle asked in a sympathetic tone.

"No. Believe me," she muttered with a cold look, "I'm used to doing everything alone." With that, the Snow Maiden zoomed away with a swirl of snow and ice chips flying up from the blades of her skates.

When she had gone, they exchanged dubious looks.

But Jake waved them over and they gathered in a huddle on one end of the room.

Archie sighed and shook his head. "We're never getting out of here, are we?"

"Yes, we are," Jake clipped out, keeping his voice low.

"I'm so tired." Dani yawned again, her green eyes watering. "We should probably rest up before the ball."

"Good idea. We need to save our strength for our escape," he agreed.

"You have a plan?" she asked in surprise.

"Sort of. Snow Maiden said she's sending out invitations to the party. That means other guests will be arriving."

"Who's she going to invite around here? Yetis?" Archie asked.

"It doesn't matter," Jake whispered impatiently. "The point is, a moment's bound to come when she's got to pay attention to her other guests. That'll be our chance to sneak away."

"Right in the middle of the party?" Dani asked.

He nodded. "The other guests will distract her."

"But then what?" Archie countered. "We're not going to get very far without a guide. We don't know where we're going."

"You're right." Jake gave a grim nod. "We need to get the elf in on our plan."

"Are you nickey in the head?" Dani whispered. "We can't trust him! What if he tricks us again? He called those yetis and nearly got us killed. He'll tell Snow Maiden our plan."

"What choice do we have?" Jake whispered. "We can't just break out of here and go wandering aimlessly across the Arctic, hoping to run into Santa before we freeze to death."

"But if you tell him we mean to escape, he could betray us—again!" Dani said. "Don't forget, he already tried to convince Snow Maiden we were spies, so she would get rid of us for him."

"Well, I think he may be reconsidering his choice of allies. It's obvious he's hating life here. Look at him." Jake nodded toward the fireplace, and the others turned to see.

Across the room, Humbug was lying on the mantel, twiddling his thumbs.

Isabelle stared at the elf, reading him as best she could. "Actually, you may be right." She tilted her head thoughtfully. "I think he's starting to see he had it pretty good before he left the North Pole."

"I'll bet," Archie said.

"Come on, let's go talk to him," Jake said. "Red?"

"Caw," the sharp-dressed Gryphon answered with a nod, confirming his readiness, should it come to another chase of the lightning-fast elf.

"Just be careful not to say too much about our plan until you make sure we can trust him," Dani murmured as they moved in a tight-knit group toward the fireplace.

"Oh, I have no intention of trusting him, believe me," Jake said. "But the fact is, we've got no chance without him. Come on."

Humbug glanced over warily at them as they approached. "What do you lot want?"

"To make a deal with you," Jake replied.

At once, Humbug sat up and swung his feet over the ledge of the mantel, leaning closer with a wary but curious stare. "What sort of deal?"

"We mean to escape. You tell on us, and I'll let my Gryphon have at you!" Jake warned him.

Red growled meaningfully at the elf, the feathers on the back of his neck bristling.

Humbug blanched. "There's no need for ugly threats, you carol-singing torturers." He eyed them warily. "What did you have in mind?"

"We're getting out of here, and we're willing to let you come with us—under certain conditions. You do seem like you've had enough of your new mistress."

"Oh, whatever gave you that idea?" he retorted, then imitated Snow Maiden in a high-pitched voice: "'Tell me a joke, Humbug! Oh, tell me another one! That's not very funny, Humbug.'" He harrumphed. "I wasn't made for telling jokes! This was not what I had in mind when I left Santa's. She's dreadful! Little brat."

"Well, you've only got yourself to blame," Jake chided. "We could have been at the North Pole by now, having a nice, hot cup of cocoa, but you had to go and betray us. Maybe now you'll sing a different tune?"

"No singing, please." Then he admitted: "I want out of here as much as you do. I've even found a door that her wooden-headed soldiers usually leave unguarded. Only I'm too small to open it by myself. Otherwise, I'd have already left."

"Good, then, we'll work together—if you promise to cooperate," Jake said. "You must admit that with all her wolves, soldiers, and bears, we stand the best chance of getting out of here alive if we work together."

"What do you want me to do?" Humbug asked suspiciously.

"Simple. We'll get the door open, but once we're free, you need to show us the way to Santa's compound. You don't have to go there with us!" Jake said before Humbug could protest. "Just don't leave us to freeze to death out there. Get us close enough to the entrance of Santa's compound so we can go the rest of the way ourselves before you head off to Halloween Town."

Humbug narrowed his eyes as he considered the proposal. "Sounds fair. But how do you intend to get us out of here without her noticing?"

"At the party tonight, we'll slip away one by one while she's distracted with her other guests. Once we're free, we'll steal one of the guest's carriages—"

"Sleighs," Dani corrected.

"Or dog sleds," Archie chimed in.

"Whatever! The point is, the minute we're out the door, we make a run for it. So, are you in or not, Humbug?"

"Dashed right I'm in." The bells on his ridiculous jester hat jingled as he jumped to his feet atop the mantel.

"You'd better not try to deceive us. My cousin here is an empath. If you try to lie to us, she'll know—and then you're Gryphon food."

"Caw," Red said with a menacing stare, while Isabelle scrutinized the elf for signs of deception.

"No tricks," Humbug muttered. "Frankly, I've had my share of tomfoolery for now."

"Aw, does that mean you don't want to work in Halloween Town anymore?" Dani taunted.

Humbug furrowed his brow and looked away without an answer, but Jake didn't care either way what the elf wanted to do.

All that mattered was escape.

"Keep your eyes open at the party tonight, all of you," he ordered, glancing around at the others. "Watch for my signal. Then you'll know it's time."

CHAPTER FOURTEEN
Go With the Floe

They rested in their rooms again, saving their strength for when the time came to slip away during the party, as planned.

Eventually, the penguins waddled back to fetch them, pecking on each of their doors and squawking an eager summons. The kids opened their chamber doors, spotted each other and Red in the hallway, and then walked together to the top of the castle staircase.

Though they did not breathe a word of their plan with the toy soldiers lurking everywhere, the nods they exchanged confirmed that everyone was ready.

Archie had his tool-bag slung over his shoulder.

The girls were ready to make a run for it, too. They had complained to the Snow Maiden that the ice skates were giving them blisters, so she had magically changed their footwear into big, fluffy boots. This would make it much easier for them to flee when they seized their moment to escape.

Red was much recovered from his earlier ordeal against the yetis. When Jake saw the warlike gleam in his golden eyes, he realized Red was ready for battle again, if it came down to it.

Jake hoped it didn't, but he gave the Gryphon a pat on his withers while the others started zooming down the ice slide next to the staircase. When everyone arrived at the bottom, the penguins led them toward the great hall, running about in a state of excitement and eagerly flapping their flightless wings.

As they approached, they could already hear the rollicking music of big, loud, frantic waltzes echoing down the hallways.

They glanced at each other in surprise and soon reached the edge of the crowded ballroom, its ice-sculpted chandeliers lit up with countless dazzling lights.

But the biggest shock came when they saw the other "guests."

It looked like a party inside Noah's Ark. All the guests were animals, except for a few decidedly creepy snowmen that had somehow come to life.

There were macaroni penguins sporting grand yellow feathers on their heads; seals in their finest spotted coats; furry arctic foxes, pure white; and wolves with big fangs, sporting elegant winter fur of gray and silver.

A few polar bears had lumbered in and were gorging themselves on vast quantities of frozen shrimp. Several festive caribou here and there had decorated their antlers with sprigs of holly for the occasion. They were bobbing their heads in time with the music while some of the other animals danced around.

Jake heard Dani gasp aloud at the sight of a pair of massive brown walruses with mustachioed whiskers and terrifying tusks.

Poor Humbug; some seal with a sense of humor was bouncing the elf on his nose. The wolves howled with laughter at this trick.

Then the Snow Maiden's chief polar bear caught sight of Jake and the others standing at the edge of the great hall. The giant, vest-wearing bear rose up onto his hind legs and narrowed his bright brown eyes at them in suspicion.

He rumbled an ominous growl, informing Her Highness that they had arrived. She whirled around on her skates, then zoomed over and made a great show of greeting them with the utmost enthusiasm in front of all her guests.

What a phony she was, Jake mused. All signs of her earlier annoyance at them had vanished now that she had an audience.

She introduced them around and chatted them up and gloated at all the attention. Soon, she was loudly recounting to her guests the story of how Jake and his friends had dealt with the yetis.

All she seemed to care about was impressing everyone.

Naturally, Ice-a-belle was doing her best to get along. "It must be frightening for all of you having such dangerous creatures as those yetis nearby."

"They are certainly unpleasant." The Snow Maiden let out a sudden gasp of excitement. "Oh! I have an idea of something else we can do tomorrow for fun!"

"What's that?" Isabelle asked.

"Tomorrow we'll go yeti hunting!"

Jake stared at her. "You must be joking."

"Not at all! It sounds exciting. My grandfather always let them be, but you've shown they can be beaten. So why should we let such nasty monsters live so close to our castle and our forest? You wolves enjoy a good hunt, don't you?" she asked her furry guests.

Not even the wolves looked overly excited about hunting abominable snowmen.

"Oh, come, it'll be excellent sport."

"What would we hunt them with?" Jake asked.

"Whatever you like. My palace guards have weapons." She nodded toward the giant toy soldiers posted along the walls.

"Fine," Jake muttered. He did not intend to be here tomorrow anyway. Still biding his time and watching for the chance to escape, he took a goblet of some fizzy, foamy blue drink off the tray of a passing penguin waiter. He took a sip and frowned with no idea what it was. Banana-flavored root beer?

In any case, when the music changed, the Snow Maiden said it was time to dance, and though Jake tried to make excuses, claiming he needed to finish his beverage, she gave him no choice.

She seized his wrist and pulled him away from the others to waltz with her, just like she had threatened earlier.

Jake cast a desperate glance over his shoulder at his friends as the Snow Maiden dragged him away. This was going to be ugly.

Fighting yetis was one thing, but he did not know how to dance. *Humiliation ahead.*

Oh, why couldn't she have picked Archie? he wondered with a silent groan. Learning how to dance was part of every proper young gentleman's education; and while Jake had been roaming the streets of London like a wild, soot-streaked heathen, Archie's tutor, Henry, had made sure the boy genius learned his way around a ballroom—at least enough not to make a fool of himself, as Jake was presently doing. Unfortunately for the Snow Maiden, she was a head taller than Archie and refused to dance with him because he would make her look like a giraffe.

Archie, however, was a good height to dance with Dani, and Jake was shocked to see how much fun those two seemed to be having waltzing around while he was in agony.

It only made him fume the more.

As the Snow Maiden threw him around the ice, Jake struggled to keep his balance and glimpsed Isabelle sitting this one out like a wallflower. One of the creepy snowmen glided over to her and bowed, suavely asking her to dance.

Her answer: she got up and walked away.

Well, Jake couldn't blame her. Snowmen were not supposed to be alive any more than gingerbread men, he thought, which brought him back to the matter at hand.

Escaping.

If they ever reached Santa's compound alive, he was going to have a serious word with the old fellow about his granddaughter, among other things.

"You're not even trying!" the Snow Maiden said in exasperation.

"Yes, I am! I told you I can't dance!"

"You're about as graceful as a walrus."

"I can't help it."

"Follow my lead!" she ordered. But just when Jake was wondering how long this torment could last, the castle doors burst open.

Without warning, a gust of sparkling snow blew in, and a blond young man, windblown and rosy-cheeked, with half a dozen gorgeous, scantily clad, angel-winged Valkryies arrayed behind him came striding down the corridor.

The music stopped, the animals gasped aloud, and everyone quit dancing, much to Jake's relief.

"*What* is going on here?" the newcomer exclaimed, scanning the ballroom.

Jake knew in an instant that he was the owner of the castle: Jack Frost.

Everyone stared at him, especially Isabelle, for the prince of winter was admittedly good looking (and as fashionably dressed as his sister). He wore a blue velvet jacket and a scarf tossed around his neck just so.

"He's soooo cool," a creepy snow-woman sighed nearby.

Jack Frost had an air of roguery about him, however. Perhaps he had inherited his grandfather's jolly sense of fun, for his blue eyes twinkled like he'd had a little too much eggnog. While the Valkyries posed and pouted behind him, his searching gaze picked his sister out of the crowd. "Well, well, having a party at my house and you didn't even invite me—" he started, then he stopped himself. "Hold on!"

His stare homed in on Jake with elder-brotherly protectiveness. "Who's that dancing with my sister?"

Aw, great, Jake thought.

"None of your business!" the Snow Maiden replied, skating in front of him. "What are you doing home, Jack?"

"Oh, surprised you, did I?" He let out a loud laugh.

She rolled her eyes. "Just take your friends and go to some other part of the castle. These are my guests and this is *my* party."

"This is *my* house," her brother said.

She stamped her foot. "You can't come in and take over my whole party!"

"I can do whatever I want," he replied, and the sibling quarrel that followed gave Jake and his friends the chance they had been waiting for—the perfect opportunity to escape.

But Jake knew they mustn't be too obvious. He turned and scanned the crowd until his eyes locked with Archie's across the room. He gave his cousin a meaningful nod.

Archie nodded back and took hold of Dani's arm, murmuring in her ear. They headed out.

Jake glanced next at Isabelle, who had been leaning by the wall; she sent him a discreet nod, backing toward the corridor. Red was already slipping away. Meanwhile, a red-and-green sparkle-trail fading off in the same direction told him Humbug had also got the message and was zipping off at elf-speed to meet them at the exit.

Everybody was accounted for...

As the Snow Maiden argued with her brother, Jake backed away with an awkward look, as though embarrassed to be caught so close to the line of fire in a family squabble.

A few of the Valkyries glanced at Jake as though they thought they recognized him, but thank goodness, as a mere lowly twelve-year-old, he thought with a scoff, he was hardly worthy of their notice.

He all but tiptoed backward while the tall, blond, Scandinavian beauties went on waving their white-feathered wings with an air of boredom, hands on hips.

Jake glanced over his shoulder toward his goal—the other hallway. But scanning the ballroom as he stole toward the exit, he saw a couple of the giant toy soldiers looking in the direction his friends had gone.

He had to cover their retreat. He knew they'd never get out of here if the soldiers decided to follow.

Heart pounding, he glanced around the ballroom looking for a solution, and seized upon the first idea that popped into his head.

Using his telekinesis, he caused a large, snow-white polar bear to drop her blue drink all over herself.

The blue-stained bear turned around with a snarl, apparently blaming the big, brown walrus standing behind her for the mishap. She roared as if to say, *"Why don't you watch where you're going?"*

The walrus lifted its tusks in warning and roared back at her. *"It wasn't me!"*

The polar bear roared outright, incensed by this defiance; the walrus headbutted her in answer.

The bear went flying backward, and in the next moment, the fight turned into a free-for-all. No wonder, thought Jake, for the room was filled with animals who usually regarded each other as predator or prey.

With the fur flying, the giant toy soldiers rushed to break up the brawl.

Jake darted out of the ballroom and raced into the corridor, confident that so far, no one even noticed they were gone.

"Jake! Problem," Archie reported as he skidded to a halt at the end of the icy hallway, where the others waited. "The door's frozen shut!"

"I'll blast it. But first..." He took off the blue sash the Snow Maiden had put on him as part of his silly Prince Charming outfit and turned to Humbug. "Come 'ere."

"What? I said I wouldn't run off!" the elf exclaimed.

"You know full well you're too fast for us. If you take off at top speed, we'll be as good as lost. We'll never keep up with you unless you are restrained. So hold still."

"Hurry! We don't have time for this!" Humbug protested.

"It would be different if you hadn't already proved yourself untrustworthy!" Jake said.

Red backed him up with a growl.

"Fine," the elf huffed. He lifted his hands, allowing Jake to tie the sash around his waist like a leash.

Archie checked his knot and tightened it a little while the sounds of the melee in the ballroom echoed down the hallway to them. Jake doubted they had more than another minute or two before the Snow Maiden realized they were gone.

"You'll need your compass," Humbug told Archie. "We're heading northwest."

Archie took it out of his tool-bag, while Jake glanced at the girls. "Ready?"

They nodded.

"Good. Stand back, then." With a moment's concentration, he summoned up his telekinesis, then fired it full force at the tall, frozen metal door. It flew off its hinges with a bang. At once, snow swirled into the hallway. "Let's go!"

Jake held tightly onto Humbug's leash as they ran out into the usual blizzard-like conditions.

Archie glanced at his compass, then pointed ahead. "That way!" he yelled over the wind.

"The woods?" Dani cried. "What about the yetis?"

"This time, no one's going to summon them," Jake said with a sharp glance at Humbug. "C'mon. The trees will give us some cover from the wind."

Knowing that the Snow Maiden and her forces could easily follow their tracks in the snow, their only hope was speed. The more distance they could put between the castle and themselves, the better off they'd be.

Desperate as they all were to escape, it felt like they were going at a snail's pace. Even with the magic spell that kept their high-fashion clothes somewhat warm, the cold numbed their limbs; the wind made breathing harder; and without Archie's snowshoes, each step was more like climbing as they sank up to their hips in snow with every stride.

It was exhausting, and after five minutes, the snowy woods still seemed no closer. They were going as fast as they could, but Humbug was beyond frustrated at having to travel so slowly.

"Hurry up!"

"Don't yell at us!" Dani warned. "You're the one who caused all this when you threw Spiteful Spice on us!"

"How f-f-far is it t-to Santa's?" Archie chattered.

"Two miles that way, once you reach the road!" Humbug pointed at the woods. "Now will you let me go?"

"Road? You must be joking," Jake said. "How are we supposed to find a road under all that snow?"

But suddenly, there was a shout behind them.

They realized they had been discovered.

"After them!" the Snow Maiden bellowed, pointing from astride her polar bear.

The kids looked back in dread to find an army of giant toy soldiers pouring out of the castle. Two long rows of the tall wooden men came goose-stepping after them, their long wooden legs allowing them to march over the deep snow as if they were on stilts.

Half a dozen wolves also burst out of the doorway and came racing after them, barking all the while.

While the soldiers were relentless, the wolves were fast. They quickly flanked the Snow Maiden's infantry lines, gaining on the kids with shocking speed. With their thick fur, the wolves were indifferent to the cold, bounding through the snow like they were born to hunt in it—which, in fact, they were.

"Head them off!" Her Highness ordered the menacing canines.

They obeyed.

Rather than attacking the kids, the wolves rushed past them and got into position ahead, blocking the way to the woods.

"What do we do?" Archie shouted. "Summon the yetis to keep them busy?"

"No!" everyone else said in unison.

"Caw!" Red flew off to keep the wolves distracted.

"Be careful!" Jake called, watching the Gryphon flap up into the sky.

Red proceeded to dive-bomb the wolves, taunting them by gliding just over their heads, lifting higher when the animals leaped up to try to catch him, their fanged jaws snapping.

While Red kept the wolves distracted, Humbug looked around. "Quick, that way!"

Following the elf's urging, they ran down the slope between the woods and the castle, helping each other along.

Jake worried about where they might end up. The Snow Maiden would not leave the road to Santa's compound unprotected.

But for now, they had no choice but to change course. It was that or get recaptured.

The twin lines of giant toy soldiers marched after them, while Red continued harrying the wolves from the air.

"Oh no!" Dani said when they found themselves coming up to the edge of the water. "We're trapped!"

"You tricked us!" Isabelle said, turning to glare at Humbug.

"I didn't, honestly!" he cried.

"Wait, look!" Jake glanced around at his feet. "We're standing on ice." At once, he drew Risker from its sheath and knelt down, slamming the blade into the ice with both hands. It cracked, but he had a long way to go. "Anything you can do," he said through gritted teeth.

"Screwdriver!" Archie plunged his hand into his tool-bag and pulled out his screwdriver, along with a hammer.

While Jake continued sawing through the ice with Risker, Archie used the screwdriver like a chisel, angling the sharp tip against the ice and banging the top of the handle with the hammer to drive it in.

Dani and Isabelle started jumping nearby, using their own weight to help widen the growing crack in the ice. They steadied each other, for it was slippery, and falling into the Arctic Sea would surely mean death in minutes.

Finally, there was a great crack, a crunch, and a splash as the piece of ice broke off along the water's edge. The girls dropped to their knees to keep from sliding off into the water as the ice floe rocked beneath them on the waves.

The boys reached out to push off the land, sending them farther out into the current.

The soldiers were on their way, with the Snow Maiden on her polar bear, giving orders like a general as she raced in their direction. "Stop them! They're getting away!" she screeched.

But she was too late.

Jake beckoned to his Gryphon. "Come on, Red! We're getting out of here!"

Red wheeled around up into the sky and flew after them.

"Caw!" Red did not like what he saw as he approached.

"Come on down, boy! It's all right." Jake watched nervously, knowing that if there was one thing Red hated, it was flying over the ocean. "You can do it! Don't be afraid!"

Somehow, the noble beast forced himself to join them, and even used his wings to propel the ice floe farther out to sea as he descended, hooking his lion claws into the ice to get a firmer grip.

Behind them, on the icy shore, the Snow Maiden bellowed in rage, but her giant toy soldiers could go no farther.

Cursing with such language that would have surely got her name put down on the top of Santa's Naughty list, she seemed half inclined to urge her polar bear into the water after them, but in the end, she didn't bother.

They drifted out to sea.

CHAPTER FIFTEEN
The Prodigal Elf

If it was freezing cold on land, the kids soon found it was unbearably frigid out on the Arctic Sea. There was nothing to break the bitter wind, and worse, the waves rocked the slippery slab of ice on which they stood, continually threatening to tilt them into the water.

They huddled together for warmth in the middle of their little floating island, holding on to Red, who kept them anchored to the ice by digging in his claws.

"We have to do something," Archie said. "We can't just drift out here until we die."

"You *are* a genius, aren't you?" Humbug muttered with his usual sarcasm.

By now, they were learning to ignore it.

"I could use my telekinesis," Jake offered uncertainly, though he had no real notion of where to aim it, what to do.

"How's t-t-that goin' help?" Dani chattered.

"I don't know!" he answered. Once again, the sheer pain of the cold was making it hard to think. Their faces stung and their limbs tingled with the first signs of frostbite.

"Let me try something," Isabelle murmured. "I think I have an idea..."

"Isabelle, come back!" Dani shouted as the older girl moved toward the edge of the ice floe, still holding her hand.

Isabelle ignored her and stared into the deep. With her blond hair blowing wildly in the sea wind, she lifted her free hand out over the water and closed her eyes with a look of concentration.

"What is she doing?" Jake whispered.

Understanding filled Archie's freckled face. "She's reaching out telepathically to any animals in the area."

"Animals? We're in the middle of the ocean," Dani said. "The last thing we need is another polar bear—"

A sudden spout of water in the distance to the starboard side of their ice floe gave the answer.

Jake smiled in relief as Archie nodded.

"Look at that. Clever girl, sis," he said. Then he glanced at Dani. "Whales aren't fish, they're mammals, remember? I guess that means she can talk to them, too."

"Lucky for us," Jake said.

Dani stifled a small cry of terror when a huge whale tail broke the surface of the water, as if the passing leviathan were waving casually at them.

The tail alone was larger than their ice floe.

"It's coming closer!" Dani hugged Red harder, clinging to the Gryphon for all she was worth.

"Of course it is. She summoned it," Archie said, peering toward the waves.

"Please tell me she knows what she's doing. That thing is gigantic. What if it swallows us like Jonah?"

"We're dead either way," Jake replied.

"Please help us!" Isabelle called aloud, for their benefit, so the others would know what she was mentally transmitting to the massive creature. "We're lost. We're just children," she added, since whales probably had a low opinion of the species that commanded the whaling vessels that roamed the seven seas. "Please, we need to get to Santa's!"

Jake and the others gasped when they heard the whale answer Isabelle. Its mysterious, ancient voice vibrated the air around them with a series of clear, submerged tones, low then high.

But even Jake, determined as he was to act brave, let out a shout of terror as the impossibly huge animal surfaced and swam up slowly behind the ice floe.

Its long, charcoal-gray back was as big as the hull of the old Viking ship they had seen in Norway.

They gripped on to each other, but there was nowhere to run.

"It's going to eat us!" Dani whimpered.

"I believe it eats plankton," Archie said in a tight voice. "A gentle giant. Right?"

"We're about to find out," Jake muttered, while Dani pulled Isabelle back from the edge.

The whale lowered its barnacled head a bit—a head the size of a carriage—and pushed the ice floe gently with its brow.

"Mother Mary," Dani whispered. "We're moving!"

"Thank you so much!" Isabelle called down to the whale in relief as their frigid floating island ceased drifting aimlessly. Instead, it headed back toward the distant outline of the land. "Not too fast, mind you!" she added anxiously. "We don't want to tip over!"

Jake's heart beat a frantic staccato, but after a few minutes, he noticed in relief that the whale was pushing them toward a spot well north of the Snow Maiden's castle. As an added benefit, the fishy-smelling breath coming out of its blowhole warmed the air around them just a bit.

"It's a good thing he knows where Santa lives," Archie said when he finally overcame his shock.

"All the arctic creatures know where Santa lives," Humbug spoke up after a moment. "They come to us when they need help."

"Us?" Jake echoed. He glanced skeptically at their little friend. "I thought you were done with all those tiresome Christmas preparations at the North Pole."

Humbug stared at him, for once with no sarcastic reply at the ready.

Jake was rather intrigued. "Provided this whale doesn't eat us, are you going to come in once we get there?"

"I don't know." Humbug's gaze fell slowly. "I'm not sure they'll let me in."

"Oh, come. Santa and Mrs. Claus put out a reward for your safe return."

"So they could punish me once they got me back!" he cried.

"Don't be silly," Jake said. "Even the Snow Maiden said Santa gives everybody second chances."

Humbug heaved a sigh. "I don't know. If I did, at the very least, I imagine I'm going to be in a lot of trouble. He'll probably put me on reindeer stall-mucking duty."

"Well, maybe you should just continue on your way to Halloween Town, then," Jake said, slanting him a shrewd look.

Humbug frowned at him.

"Would you really rather dedicate your life to scaring people instead of spreading Christmas cheer?" Dani asked.

"Scaring people's fun! Besides, people are a pain! They deserve it," Humbug insisted, but he did not look as convinced about the whole thing as before.

"Well, suit yourself," Jake said, but when he glanced at Isabelle, she gave him a knowing smile.

It did not take an empath to see that, despite his protests, Humbug was truly torn about what to do.

"Whoa, look at that!" Archie pointed toward the land.

They were approaching the narrow, rounded entrance to an ice-cave, like a tunnel in the glacier.

"Of course!" Humbug murmured, recognizing it. "The whale's taking us to the runway."

"What is that?" Jake asked.

"The tunnel Santa drives the sleigh through on Christmas Eve when it's time for takeoff. He returns through it, too."

"You mean we're almost there? At the North Pole?" Dani exclaimed.

"You're looking at it," Humbug replied, nodding at the broad, snow-covered hill that bulged up, dome-like, just behind the glacier.

"I don't see anything," Jake murmured in amazement, scanning the landscape before him as the whale pushed them ever nearer to the icy shore.

"No, you wouldn't, would you?" Humbug said. "That's the whole point. The Great Igloo is perfectly camouflaged for its surroundings. Warm, too. You'll feel better once we get inside."

"We?" Archie asked pointedly.

But Humbug merely frowned and still wouldn't give an answer about his intentions.

At last, the floating ice floe bumped up against the frozen edge at the entrance to the tunnel. They jumped off and thanked the whale profusely, waving farewell.

The whale answered in kind as it dove deeper to somersault underwater, turning back out toward the open sea; its huge tail surfaced, flicking them with sea foam that froze instantly on their clothes as it waved goodbye.

"What a wonderful creature," Isabelle breathed. "I shall never be talked into wearing a whalebone corset after that."

"Me neither," Dani said.

Jake looked askance at her with a bit of a smirk, amused at the thought of the tomboyish carrot-head ever being grown up enough to need a lady's corset, of all things.

"I reckon we go this way?" Archie pointed up the mysterious ice tunnel. Now that they were sheltered from the wind, his usual cheer was quick to return. "I can't believe we're about to meet Santa! Hurry up!"

"Well, Humbug? Are you coming, or is this where we part ways? You're small enough to slip out around the edge of the tunnel entrance there. If you want to go, we won't stop you, true to our word. Of course, that means I can't collect the reward. It's too bad," Jake said. "That wish would have meant a great deal to someone out there."

"Who?" the elf shot back with a defensive scowl.

"A six-year-old boy I know named Petey."

"Who is he to you?" Humbug asked, trying once more to sound sarcastic—but failing.

Jake couldn't answer the question. His voice had evaporated at the thought of his young friend spending yet another Christmas in that dreary place.

Staring at Jake, Dani answered for him. "Petey was a kid at the orphanage with Jake. Practically worshiped him."

"Orphanage, you say?" Humbug echoed as his eyes widened slowly.

Jake cleared his throat and looked away. "Well, it's your choice."

Humbug stared down the tunnel. "I guess I could just show you where the elevator is." He turned away impatiently. "Well, come on, if you're coming!"

The grumpy elf trudged off ahead of them.

They exchanged surprised glances that Humbug had not fled yet. Then they followed him.

As they walked up the dim, bluish ice tunnel, Dani turned to Jake, wearing a smile from ear to ear. "I'm so proud of you!"

"Oh, shut up," he mumbled with a blush.

She laughed. "I figured out your wish."

"Don't say it! You might nix it."

Not that Santa was going to give him the reward unless Humbug willingly chose to turn himself in. After all, Jake had given his word to let the elf go if he'd cooperate.

Soon, the tunnel ended in a formidable pair of tall iron doors, but cattycorner to them stood a smaller pair of shiny brass ones.

The latter turned out to be the elevator, which they discovered when Humbug pushed the button set into the wall beside it at elf-height, down around their knees.

"What's through there?" Archie asked, nodding at the big doors while they waited for the elevator.

"That's the doorway for the sleigh to come through," Humbug said. "The reindeer training area is behind it, and the stables. Reindeer give off a surprising amount of heat. They live on the lower floor beneath us because of course heat rises. Just another way we keep the place warm."

"I see."

The elevator doors opened with a *bing!*

They stepped in and immediately noticed Christmas music playing softly. Humbug winced; Jake and Archie glanced at the elf and each other in amusement.

Then the brass doors slid shut, and the elevator trundled upward into the great dome.

Humbug seemed nervous about what sort of punishment he might receive for deserting his post. But as the elevator rose, and the threat of doom faded behind them, the kids grew breathlessly excited to see Santa's famous operation.

Few people ever did.

Jake's heart pounded, and—he could not help himself—as soon as the elevator glided to a stop, he rushed out the moment the brass doors parted.

The others followed suit.

"Wait for me!" Humbug said in annoyance.

But the four of them had already crossed the red-carpeted waiting area outside the bank of elevators. They reached the brass railing that overlooked the huge, open area below and stared in amazement.

Nobody said a word.

As the warmth flooded back into their frozen extremities, they watched the busy scene before them, speechless with wonder.

Jake could not believe he was just one flight of stairs away from the global headquarters of Christmas itself.

"Do you see him anywhere?" Dani whispered, scanning the crowd.

"No." Jake knew that she meant Santa Claus, of course.

"It's so beautiful," Isabelle murmured.

"Blast it, can't see." Archie took off his spectacles, which were fogging up now that he'd come inside where it was warm.

Jake didn't even want to blink to avoid missing any of the astonishing sights.

Christmas trees decorated every way a person could imagine ringed the wide-open space. The pillars that held up the dome of Santa's Great Igloo were candy-striped, the air smelled of cinnamon pinecones, and the whole place was crawling with elves, who sped about at their duties, kicking up red-and-green sparkles as they worked. They were stacking brightly wrapped boxes into seven towers, headed, Jake guessed, for each of the seven continents.

But leave it to Archie to ask the logical question. For when the boy genius put his de-fogged glasses back on, he frowned in his particular, thoughtful way. "How in the world is Santa going to fit all those presents on his sleigh? Physics makes the whole thing quite impossible."

"Magic sack, obviously," Humbug answered. "The presents appear in the sack just when they should, one house, one family at a time."

"Really?" Dani exclaimed.

"Well, it's the only sensible way to do it, isn't it? He's not going to carry that whole mess with him halfway round the world all night. He's an old man. Think about it!"

"Ohhh," they said.

"Besides, that's how he sees everybody," Humbug mumbled. "Not countries' worth, not by the thousands. Individuals. That's how he knows which list to put you on."

"So he knows everybody? How?" Jake asked skeptically.

"No idea," Humbug said with a shrug. "He just does."

The elf fell silent, gazing at the everyday goings-on of the life he had left behind.

Isabelle looked askance at him. "How proud you must've been to be part of all this."

"Yes, but he wasn't joking," Dani said. "This does look like a *ton* of work."

Humbug seemed to struggle for words. "It is. But...you know, like Santa always says..."

"What does he say?" Jake pursued, arching a brow.

"That it's better to give than to receive." Even as he said the words, Humbug melted. Staring at the busy scene below, two big tears welled up in his eyes as he realized how wrong he had been.

The elf's whole expression changed.

His wizened face softened with kindliness, his cheeks grew rosy, and a glow of gratitude stole into his eyes, mingling with the tears of regret there. Most shocking of all, a tremulous smile began to spread across his grumpy little mouth.

"Humbug?" Jake asked gently. "Are you all right?"

"I *do* want to go back!" he burst out with a sniffle. "Even if Santa does put me on reindeer stall-mucking duty. This is my home. This is where I belong, and besides, whoever heard of a Halloween elf?" He no sooner said the words than, all of a sudden, the Snow Maiden's makeover spell broke, poofing him back magically into his Christmas elf clothes. "Ha, ha!" He looked down at himself in amazement.

At that moment, one of the other elves saw him standing there. "Humbug?" The other elf stopped in his tracks. He pointed at him. "Look, everybody! Humbug's back!"

Everybody looked.

When the elves saw their missing comrade standing there, joy flooded over their little, long, pointy-nosed faces. They abandoned their work with eager shouts of relief and came rushing over, scores of them.

"Oh, Humbug! You're all right! We thought you were dead!"

As the elves stampeded toward them, barely taking notice of the children, Jake leaned down to Humbug and whispered behind his hand: "Maybe there's no need to bother Santa with the details of your little Halloween Town plan."

"Really?" Humbug asked hopefully.

He nodded. "We'll forget about all that, if you will."

The elf gazed at him gratefully. "Thank you, Lord Griffon. You're not actually half bad."

Then the swarm of excited elves flooded onto the landing, crowding around and cheering that their missing mate had returned, safe and sound.

"Everyone will be so relieved to hear you're alive! Santa's going to want to throw a party when he sees that you're all right!"

"We elves do love a party," a small gent in a green coat informed the staring children.

Then another little fellow threw his arm around Humbug's shoulder. "Let's go tell the boss you're back!"

But they didn't even have to.

On the next landing up, a door marked 'OFFICE' banged open. A fat old man with a white beard rushed out and peered over the brass railing.

Dani gasped aloud.

All the elves pointed eagerly to Humbug.

"Look, sir—look who's come back!"

Humbug stared up at his former employer in chastened uncertainty. Jake held his breath, wondering if Humbug would be immediately punished or if the 'boss' would accept his runaway elf back at all.

But while Jake braced himself for Santa's wrath, the red-suited man boomed out a short, jolly laugh, then he came bounding down the steps with the agility of a much younger (and slimmer) man.

"Ho, ho, Humbug! Sweet snowfields, you're safe!" Before the elf could protest, the big man scooped him up in a Santa-sized hug.

CHAPTER SIXTEEN
Santa Central

"Well now, Humbug, who's this you've brought to see us?" Santa rumbled, releasing the chastened elf from his bear-hug. Rosy-cheeked and beaming, the old man wiped away a quick tear of happiness over his missing elf's return.

His show of emotion astonished Jake. Clearly, the towering fellow was just an old softie.

Santa looked from Humbug to them, then he gave the elf a nudge. "Manners, shortling. Aren't you going to introduce me to your friends?"

Dani furrowed her brow and leaned to whisper in Jake's ear: "If Santa really knows everyone, why's he asking who we are? Shouldn't he already know?"

The jolly old elf laughed aloud, overhearing, much to Dani's horror. "Ho, ho, I was only being polite, Daniela Catherine!" he said merrily. "Some people find it off-putting, you see, that I already know so much about them before we're introduced."

Dani turned as red as Santa's trousers and stammered, "Sorry."

Jake did not envy her in that moment. He made a mental note to keep his sarcastic comments to a minimum, for it seemed that Father Frost had terribly sharp ears for such an old man.

Santa waved off the carrot-head's embarrassment with one of his big, callused hands. "It's all right, lass. Never fear, your spot on the Nice list is secure, my dear Dani O'Dell."

"Whew," she said under her breath.

"And how is that funny little dog of yours? What's his name...? Ah—Teddy!" he suddenly remembered.

Dani was astonished. "Yes, Santa, Teddy is his name. He's doing well, sir. Th-thank you for asking."

"Give him my best."

"I-I definitely will," Dani said in wonder.

"So then." Now that it was out in the open that no introductions were actually necessary, his twinkly blue eyes traveled across their faces with fond amusement. "Here are the young heroes I should thank for bringing my lost elf safely back to me. Gentle-hearted Miss Isabelle; brilliant Master Archie; brave Lord Jake; steadfast Miss Dani; and, of course, the renowned Claw the Courageous."

"Becaw." Red gave Santa one of his noblest bows.

"Welcome, Crafanc-y-Gwrool. An honor to finally meet you, as well." Santa bowed back to the Gryphon while the children beamed and stood a little taller, warmed indeed by such wonderful compliments on the very heart of who they each were.

"You understand Red, Santa?" Isabelle asked in surprise, looking from the old man to the Gryphon. "You can talk to animals, too?"

"Why, my dear, they are among some of my most interesting acquaintances," he declared with a wink.

"Mine, too!" she answered.

"Ahem, so, right," Jake said, ready to get down to business. "I believe we saw a notice in the *Clairvoyant*, sir. Something about a Christmas wish to be granted as a reward for bringing Humbug back?"

He laughed merrily at Jake's brisk reminder. "To be sure. I take it you're the one who'd like to claim the wish, m'boy?"

"I am, sir," he said boldly.

"Very well. We will see right to it. But first, I, er, see you've met my granddaughter." He glanced down at their strange, high-fashion clothes. "My apologies if Snowy was at all…unpleasant to you. She's a good girl, really. Mrs. Claus says she's simply going through a wee bit of a rebellious phase."

"You can say that again," Archie muttered under his breath.

"She didn't harm you?" Santa asked in concern.

"No, sir. She might have at the end there," Jake informed him, "but we got away."

"Ah, but of course you did." He held his round belly as he let out a broad laugh. His humor was infectious. "I daresay the five of you together are quite unstoppable. Still, she can be such a bully." Santa shook his head. "Takes after her aunt, you know. My elder sister,"

Santa added, almost whispering with a glance over his shoulder. "The Blue Hag of Winter."

Dani nodded. "We heard about her."

"Well!" Santa declared. "I will not tolerate my granddaughter following in the Winter Witch's footsteps. I shall certainly pay a visit to the castle and have a very stern word with her about her behavior."

"Don't be too hard on her, Santa," Archie spoke up. "She's just really, really bored."

"Hmm, I will take that under advisement, Master Archie. For now, the least I can do is try to make it up to you by putting you back the way you were. Unless you prefer these, er, modern fashions?"

"Oh, no, please do put us back!" Isabelle said in relief. "That is— if you don't mind, we'd be ever so grateful, sir."

"Certainly, my dear." Santa chuckled. "I wasn't sure. I can never tell what strange new thing you young people will be wearing from one year to the next."

Fine talk coming from a man in a red suit, Jake thought. But for his part, he'd be glad to be rid of the Prince Charming look.

Then Santa snapped his fingers, and gold sparkles flew out from his hand. The tiny lights traveled toward the kids, leaving trails like glowing tendrils.

The tiny golden-orange lights wrapped around each one of them and whirled around their bodies from head to toe, swirling faster, round and round, until...

Poof!

Suddenly, they were back in their own clothes.

"Ha!" To Jake's relief, his hair flopped right back over his eyebrow where it should be. His frosty ski-jump hairdo was no more. With a habitual toss of his head, he flipped his forelock out of his eyes so he could see.

Then he turned to look at the others and grinned.

"Aw, where's your purple hair?" he teased Dani.

She brought a length of her hair in front of her eyes to make sure it was back to its usual orangey autumn red.

She laughed in relief along with the others. Everyone was glad to be looking like their normal selves again. They thanked Santa for putting them back, but he had things to do.

"Children, I must have a brief meeting with Mr. Humbug. I believe we still have a few matters to sort out."

"Uh-oh," one of the other Christmas elves said in a small voice. Scores of them were still crowding around, looking on.

Humbug lowered his head.

"You shortlings need to get back to work," Santa chided. "We're on a schedule here, or have you forgotten Christmas is less than twelve hours away? Mrs. Claus catches you loitering like this..."

He didn't need to finish the sentence.

They swarmed back to their duties.

"Except for you, Crystal!" Santa called.

A knee-high girl elf with a white pom-pom on the end of her hat stopped and came back. "Yes, boss?" she asked in a squeaky little voice.

Santa held up his finger to signal her politely to wait, and turned to Jake. "This won't take long. As soon as I'm done speaking to Humbug, you and I can have our meeting about your reward. Till then, Crystal will lead you all to the kitchens."

The girl elf nodded, hearing her assignment.

"Mrs. Claus will give you a nice snack while you wait. You are our guests. Please make yourselves at home." Then Santa turned to Humbug and gestured toward the office. "Shall we?"

"Yes, sir," Humbug said obediently, head down.

Good luck, Dani mouthed at him.

"This way, please!" Crystal beckoned cheerfully. "If we hurry, we can still catch the train!"

"Train?" they murmured to one another, but there was no time to waste. They ran after Crystal, who whooshed down the few stairs off the landing and started to zip off ahead of them with the same blinding speed Humbug had demonstrated in the bakery.

"Wait!" Dani cried.

"Oh, sorry! I forgot—human speed." She giggled self-consciously and stopped to wait for them.

Although she slowed down from there, the kids still had to hurry to keep up. Jake wondered how the speedy elves avoided tripping in their curly-toed shoes.

Crystal led them around the perimeter of the huge, domed gift-sorting area in which they had first arrived.

On the far side of the room, they followed her through a tunnel of giant candy canes just as a small, brightly painted passenger train came chugging around a bend in the hallway to their left, heading toward their stop. The steam whistle blew and the train began to slow.

"Gift Sorting!" called the conductor, riding on the engine seat in front. He was a plump elf dressed in green overalls, and tipped his striped hat to Crystal as the train glided to a halt. "Welcome, guests!"

When the quaint, indoor train stopped, some elves jumped off the little open train cars and others jumped on.

"Come, VIPs sit up front." Crystal beckoned them into the first train car, which was slightly larger than the elf-sized ones behind it.

"Where you headed?" the conductor asked.

"Kitchen," Crystal told him.

"Have you there in no time. All aboard!" he called one more time, blowing the whistle to summon any other elves who needed to get to another part of the Great Igloo.

None came, so off they went.

The kids (and the Gryphon) stared in wonder at all the fascinating departments they passed as the train wound through Santa's elaborate North Pole operation.

Given that the elevator had spit them out in GIFT SORTING, the last stop before the presents were delivered, they viewed the various steps in reverse order as the train made its rounds.

For example, before the presents could be sorted, of course they had to be wrapped. GIFT WRAPPING had miles of colorful paper on spools and long tables where the elves were hard at work, judging just the right length of paper to cut and making perfect creases on every box in sight.

Next door was the BOW DEPARTMENT, where elves tied ribbons into perfect bows and handed them up to doves, who flew off over the wall divider into GIFT WRAPPING, and dropped them onto the presents, just where they were needed.

Farther down the tracks came a dizzying array of workrooms dedicated to the making to various types of presents: DOLLS, DOLL WARDROBE, DOLL FURNITURE, DOLL HOUSES, STUFFED ANIMALS, BALL DEPARTMENT, SPORTS EQUIPMENT, JUMP ROPES, ART SUPPLIES, TELESCOPES, SCIENTIFIC TOYS, EDUCATIONAL TOYS, FIGURINES, MUSIC BOXES, BOOKS, TOY PAINTING DEPARTMENT, CARPENTRY.

Archie pointed eagerly at the next workroom, where elf scientists and engineers in white lab coats and goggles were discussing their sketches of strange toys on large chalkboards.

"RESEARCH AND DEVELOPMENT?" he read aloud.

"Toys of the future." Crystal nodded sagely.

"Look, PUPPIES!" Dani pointed into the next room, a large, loud but cozy kennel, where a dozen elves were trying to contain the yipping, tail-wagging, floor-soiling, irresistible puppies running and tumbling around. The kids laughed, watching the elves chase the puppies about, trying to capture them so they could be tucked into Christmas stockings for delivery to their new owners.

KITTENS came next, and you can imagine the trouble it caused when one of these escaped (as kittens tend to do) into the area for PUPPIES.

Across the hallway was a glassed-in overlook onto the REINDEER TRAINING arena below, according to the sign. Then they saw the proof of it and gasped as a reindeer leaped up off the sawdust track and flew up past the glass, and higher, into the open space under the high dome.

It circled around and was followed by another. Santa's famous reindeer were doing a few laps to exercise their legs ahead of their marathon night of delivering toys. The kids marveled, watching the reindeers' galloping strides in midair.

But the indoor train chugged on, past a section of rooms grouped under a hanging sign above the tracks that said DECORATIONS. On the right was GARLANDS & WREATHS. Across from it was FLOWERS, with endless rows of bright poinsettias and lush amaryllis growing under warm lamps. Elves in garden gloves misted their blooms with little squeeze bottles and made sure to talk to the plants, telling them how pretty they were.

The next department kept its glass door shut because, though shielded from the wind, its back wall was open to the elements. Jake's eyes widened as he read the placard over the door: WHITE CHRISTMAS.

"I thought Jack Frost handled all the snow," he said.

"Well, he's young, you know boys in their teens…he's just a wee bit casual about showing up on *time*," Crystal said discreetly. "Santa likes to keep his own backup supply of Christmas Eve snow, just in case."

"I see," Jake murmured, then he stared once more into the snowy, half-outdoor workshop, where, instead of elves, two dozen snowmen were busy with scissors, cutting out special snowflakes just for Christmas Eve.

The train rolled on, slow and steady, on its tidy little tracks. They were getting down to the end of the line now, only a few departments left.

The next stop was the SLEIGH STATION, where mechanically minded elf driving experts were tuning up Santa's massive sleigh.

They were balancing its weight on a large mechanical platform that mimicked wind conditions. It rocked and bucked and tilted to and fro. The greasy mechanical elves didn't even look over when the train stopped to let more elves on or off. Wrapped up in work they obviously loved, they shut off the mechanical platform and agreed they needed more wax on the sleigh's runners.

During this short break, a few of them jumped up onto the sleigh to polish its already-spotless brass fittings. Others shined up its lanterns. Still others nearby rubbed saddle oil into the harnesses to keep the leather soft and supple so it would not chafe the reindeer.

"Busy, busy," Dani said, staring at them.

But the SLEIGH STATION was nothing compared to the beehive of activity going on in the very next department, titled MAILROOM.

Here, twenty elves rushed around collecting long, narrow, winding strands of paper from the ticker-tape machines that ran constantly, spitting out the endless requests from children around the world, telling Santa what they wanted for Christmas.

"Look at all these last-minute gifts! How can they only be making up their minds now?" a harried elf cried, as the ticker-tape curled around him like a friendly paper snake. "They know we're coming every year, and they only decide what they want on the afternoon of Christmas Eve? Ahh!" He fell over as the ticker-tape kept winding around him, flailing about with muffled cries, until the others hurried over to roll him out.

But Jake and his companions had gone silent at the news the elf had blurted out. They had lost all track of time, and now it was already the afternoon of Christmas Eve.

They looked around at each other in dismay, but no one dared say it aloud. *We're going to miss Christmas.* There was no way they could get back home in time to share the holiday with Great–Great Aunt Ramona and Lord and Lady Bradford—or with Henry and Helena, for that matter.

"Poor Teddy," Dani murmured. "He's going to be all alone."

"Poor us," Archie answered. "Aunt Ramona's going to kill us for ruining the village pageant. The Nativity, remember? Vicar's going to be out of luck. No Mary, no Joseph, no angel, and only *two* wise men."

Jake's heart sank as he realized he had ruined Christmas for more people than Humbug ever could.

"Becaw," Red offered.

"Quite right." Isabelle nodded at the Gryphon, then she turned to the others. "You mustn't give up hope. Santa might still have a way."

"Maybe that sleigh is fast enough to take us home and then dash back here in time for takeoff," Archie said.

"I doubt it," Jake mumbled.

But his cousin glanced back longingly toward the Sleigh Station. "I wouldn't mind taking a ride in that little beauty, I can tell you."

The girls just looked at him.

The last stop before Mrs. Claus's kitchen was the Candy Factory. Normally, Jake would have dropped everything to go in there, but the realization about missing Christmas had put a damper on his mood.

Isabelle nudged him, sensing his emotions. "Smile, coz. At least we're alive."

After the yetis, the polar bears, the wolves, the creepy wooden soldiers, and the brush with hypothermia, he had to admit, she made a good point.

So he tried.

At last, the train rolled to a halt. The conductor gave the whistle a toot, and Crystal smiled at them. "Here's your stop!" she chirped.

Jake glanced up at the sign over the arched doorway: Mrs. Claus's Kitchen. His companions were already climbing off the train. Crystal came along to introduce them to Santa's wife.

Jake jumped off the train and waved in thanks to the conductor. As he turned toward the delicious smells floating out of the kitchen, he was suddenly very eager to find out what sort of snacks Mrs. Claus might have to offer them.

He hurried after his friends.

CHAPTER SEVENTEEN
The Missus

C rystal led them through the arched doorway into Mrs. Claus's large, cozy kitchen, where they paused, taking in the heavenly smells—and controlled chaos—of the place.

The kitchen elves were hard at work everywhere, painting cookies, rolling dough, whisking eggs, washing dishes, drying them. Some splashed buckets of glaze over carrot cakes fresh out of the oven; others shook chocolate sprinkles over rows of pastries spread out over yet another worktable. One elf scampered up a ladder precariously propped against a giant spice rack as tall as a bookcase, laden with countless labeled jars.

But the dominant figure amidst all this hubbub was Mrs. Claus herself. There was no mistaking her, the female equivalent of Santa. Tall, broad, and sturdy, she wore a red dress with the sleeves rolled up, a white apron, and black boots. Her snow-white hair was piled atop her head like a dollop of whipped cream, adorned with a sprig of holly. Little glasses were perched on the bridge of her nose, and her hands were encased in giant oven mitts.

She gave the impression of smooth, sedate control, but in fact, she was in constant motion, a whirlwind of a woman who could have put a house brownie in awe.

She didn't miss a beat, giving orders that sounded like dulcet-toned requests, and making her rounds as clockwork cooking timers went off constantly with a series of shrill *dings!*

She broke an egg with one hand and mixed a batter with the other, handed the job off to an elf, then fixed a drip of white frosting on a gingerbread man where one of the painting elves had botched it. From there, she glided over to a potbellied stove and lifted the lid for a peek into a huge cauldron. "Pudding's finally boiling."

Ding!

Another timer chimed, but an elf hurried to take the next batch of meringues out of the oven for her. "I'll get it, Mrs. Claus. You've got visitors."

"I do?" She spun around and gasped in delight when she saw them. "Children! You made it! At last." She clapped her oven mitt-padded hands together and rushed toward them, where they still lingered uncertainly in the doorway. "Oh, come in, come in, my dear half-frozen little dears! Thank goodness you are safe!"

Without warning, she grabbed all four kids at once into a big, warm, grandmotherly hug and laughed, giving them a group squeeze before she released them.

None of them were used to such shows of affection and weren't quite sure what to make of it, or of her.

"Now then. Your snack is almost ready. Mr. C. told me you were on the way. And the Gryphon, too! Oh, aren't you a handsome beastie!" She took off an oven mitt to give Red a doting pat on the head.

He looked charmed in spite of himself.

"Well now, don't just stand there in the doorway!" she chided. "Come in. Sit, sit, children. There, at the table by the fire."

"We don't wish to be in your way, ma'am," Isabelle said. "You seem very busy."

"Not at all, sweeting! Nothing I can't handle with my eyes closed after all these years. It's all in the planning, you see." With a bright chuckle, she pointed at her chalkboard calendar on the back wall, which had jobs written out for every day of the year.

"Blimey," said Jake. "That's daunting."

Indeed, Mrs. Claus was remarkably calm for one of the busiest women on the earth. Here it was, with Christmas right around the corner, and she was prepared to stop everything to give them some food.

"Now then. Your snacks are almost ready. Oh, here—put a bit of this on your hands and faces while you're waiting." She fished a small bottle of something out of her apron pocket. "It's anti-frostbite cream, just in case. You young ones aren't used to our *brisk* arctic weather, I fear. Off you go." She shooed them past the elves' main workspace to a cozy kitchen table that stood atop a braided cottage rug before the crackling fireplace.

The kids had barely finished rubbing the anti-frostbite cream on their noses, cheeks, and hands, when another timer went *ding!*

"Ah, that will be your snacks." A moment later, Mrs. Claus carried over a large tray with five covered dishes and handed them out.

When Jake took the lid off his plate, his eyes misted with pleasure. Great Scott, if Mrs. Claus considered a plate piled with roast beef, gravy, and mashed potatoes a mere "snack," then he had clearly discovered utopia.

Of course, one didn't grow a Santa-sized belly eating celery, so maybe he shouldn't have been surprised.

She pulled the lid off Red's plate for him and wiped her hands on her apron. "Need anything else?"

They said no and thanked her dazedly.

"Eat up!" She beamed at them and went back to work.

"I love her," Jake whispered to the others. "Do you think they'd let me live here?"

"What, in the North Pole?" Dani asked.

"No, right in this very kitchen."

"You are a life-support system for a stomach, coz," Archie said.

Jake grinned, then they dug in to their pre-Christmas feast.

Mrs. Claus came back a little later to check on them. She was so happy to see them enjoying her cooking that she took a short break from her nonstop work and stayed to chat, leaning against a chair. "So, how is poor Humbug? And how was our Snow Maiden when you saw her? I do worry about her so. Oh, I see—can't talk with your mouths full. What well-mannered children! Perhaps you were a good influence on Snowy. Did you get to meet Jack? Isn't he charming? Takes after his grandfather, that handsome rascal. You should've known Santa when he was younger." Mrs. Claus gave them a mischievous wink. "He was a wild one. Oh, but I straightened him out once I got hold of him, believe you me."

The children glanced at each other, tickled by this unexpected revelation.

She bustled off and brought them the perfect dessert, something not too sweet after their overindulgence on Marie's French pastries—a plate full of lemon biscuits, washed down with a hot cup of peppermint tea.

When Jake finished these, he flopped back in his chair, feeling happy and extremely lazy. "Mrs. Claus," he declared, "you're never getting rid of me."

She laughed. "You're a little tall for an elf, but if you insist, I'm sure we can find you a job making toys. Of course, that's a craft that takes time to learn. You might have to start out by shoveling snow. What do you think?"

"No, ma'am, there's only one job that I'll consider: official food taster for the North Pole."

"Why, so you can be as fat as Santa?" she teased.

But Jake's playful decision to move into Mrs. Claus's kitchen was cut short, for a moment later, he was summoned to Santa's office.

It was time to see about his reward.

CHAPTER EIGHTEEN
A Sprinkling of Sugar

"Sir?"

Arriving in the doorway of the office, Jake found Santa seated at his desk. He could barely see him behind the stacks of thick ticker-tape loops, apparently sent up from the Mailroom.

With his spectacles perched on his nose, the old man was sorting the Christmas wishes into several bins variously marked Approved, Maybe Next Year, and Absolutely Not!

"Ahem. You sent for me, sir?"

Santa looked up and grinned brightly. "Ah, there you are, my boy! Come in. I trust you had a nice visit with the Missus?"

"She is first rate," Jake declared as he shut the office door behind him.

Santa chuckled. "Ah, yes, everybody loves the Missus. The power behind the throne," he added with a wink. "Well, m'boy! No time to lose. Let's get down to business, shall we, in the matter of your reward." Santa gestured to the chair on the other side of his desk.

Jake walked over and eagerly took a seat.

"As promised, for the safe return of my poor, misguided Humbug, one Christmas wish granted—whether I approve or not, no questions asked. Have you had a chance to figure out what you want?" Santa asked, taking a sip of his hot cocoa.

"Yes, sir."

"Good. Come and tell me in my ear." Santa put his mug down and beckoned him around the desk with a businesslike flick of his white-gloved fingers.

Heart pounding, Jake rose and stepped around the desk. He felt a little silly—this seemed an exercise for little kids—but with a real

Christmas wish at stake, he was not taking any chances.

He leaned down and whispered his request in Santa's ear.

"Hmm," the old man said.

Jake straightened up again and stepped back, nervously trying to read Santa's reaction. It was hard to judge his expression behind the big, snowy beard.

"Hmm," he said again. Then he glanced shrewdly at Jake. "I'm impressed. That's a good wish." Santa nodded, studying him. "A very good wish, actually. That's what you want? You're sure?"

"Yes, sir."

"Interesting. Very interesting indeed."

"Can you do it?"

"Course I can." Santa gave him a don't-insult-me glance. "It's done."

Jake's eyebrows shot up. "That's it?"

His blue eyes twinkled behind his wire-rimmed spectacles. "Look into the matter after Christmas morning if you doubt me. I think you will be pleased. Now then, since you've proven yourself such a reliable young man, leading your friends through such treacherous dangers, I wonder if I might ask you for a favor?"

"Me? Certainly, I'd be honored."

"Good lad!" Santa rose from his desk. "I wouldn't normally bother a civilian with something like this. It's just we're in the final countdown to Christmas, and I find myself a little short on time. But steps must be taken, and quickly, to reverse the effects of that nasty Spiteful Spice our little friend sprinkled all over those poor bakeries."

"Humbug confessed?" Jake asked in surprise. "Fancy that. We said we wouldn't tell on him."

"And that was very generous of you, considering how horrid he was to you all. But no. He didn't have to tell me what he'd done. I already knew." With a low chuckle, Santa tapped the side of his nose in the age-old sign of secrecy, then he moved around his desk and headed toward the fireplace.

"Blimey," Jake murmured, turning in his chair. Santa really did seem to know everything about everybody. "How can I help?"

"One moment and I'll show you." With heavy footfalls Santa strode across the room and lifted a large and very pretty snow globe off the mantel.

It looked familiar. Then Jake realized he had seen a matching one in Mrs. Claus's kitchen. He watched curiously as Santa gave it a shake and made the "snow" inside it fly.

Setting it back on the mantel, which was at eye level with him, Santa pressed the brass button on the front of the snow globe's painted wooden base. Under the button, the little plaque said: PUSH TO CALL. He leaned toward the snow globe and said loudly: "Come in, Lollipop! This is Midnight Flier. Do you read me?"

Mrs. Claus's face suddenly appeared in the snow globe.

"Right here, dear." Busy managing her domain, she stepped into view drying her hands on a dish towel. Jake could see parts of her kitchen behind her, and was intrigued to realize the enchanted snow globes were some sort of communication device. "What can I do for you, love?"

"I need that, uh...oh, what's it called?" He cast about. "The fluffy, white, powdery stuff. In the jar. The doctor what's-his-name concoction? It's on the tip of my tongue—"

"The Dr. Starshine's," she said, as though reading his mind.

He snapped his fingers. "That's the one!"

She smiled. "On its way." Mrs. Claus gestured to an elf to bring it to him at once. Then she turned back to Santa. "Anything else, dear?"

"Better send the young'uns to the parlor, Lolli. Master Jake and I are almost done here."

"Oh, what did he wish for?" Mrs. Claus asked in suspense.

"Tell you all about it over supper. What are we having, by the way?"

"Your favorite. Roast beef."

"Hello, Mrs. Claus!" Jake waved to her in the background.

"Hello again, Jake! Oh, sorry! Pudding's boiling over. Lollipop out!" She reached toward her snow globe and pressed the button, and the image inside the glass ball disappeared.

"Clever device," Jake remarked.

"Yes, they're very handy." Santa had no sooner turned away from the snow globe when there was a knock on the door.

At about knee level.

Blazes, thought Jake. He knew by now that Christmas elves were fast, but even Santa looked surprised at how quickly the elf had arrived from Mrs. Claus's kitchen on the far end of the Great Igloo. He answered the door, bending down to take the concoction from his little helper.

A moment later, he returned, carrying a red and white striped jar with a silver metal lid. "Here we are. Dr. Starshine's Delightful Elven Dusting Sugar. It's very simple to use. Just flip the metal spout up on the lid and shake some of this stuff on anyone or anything Humbug might've tainted with the Spiteful Spice."

"What does it do?"

"Turns them sweet, of course. But you must see to this task as soon as you possibly can. The longer the Spiteful Spice sits, the more it soaks in, the more powerful it becomes, and the nastier the effects."

"I'll do it right away, sir, as soon as I get back to London. Though...I don't know exactly when that might be."

"Ha! Come with me. We'll get you home tonight."

"Really?" Jake's eyes widened. He jumped up eagerly out of his chair. "How?"

"You'll see. Let's go meet your friends in the parlor."

Santa finished the last gulp of his hot chocolate and headed for the door. Jake trailed after him but hung back, hesitating slightly.

This was his only chance to ask Santa the painful question that had long troubled him. "Can I ask you something, Santa?"

The old man paused halfway to the door and turned around. "Of course. What is it, lad?"

Jake faltered. "I didn't really like you in the past. Because it seemed like you always forgot about kids like me."

Sadness wreathed his lined face. "My dear boy."

Jake swallowed hard. As difficult as this was, he had to ask, for his fellow orphans' sake. And his own. "Why didn't you ever come? To the orphanage, I mean. Was it because we were all too bad to be given any presents? Were we on the Naughty list? I mean, I for one probably deserved it, but the little ones, like Petey..."

"No, no, no. Oh, my dear lad." Santa came toward him with a pained look. "I'm so sorry you felt forgotten, Jake. But the truth is, I did come. I was there. Every year, without fail."

"What?" Jake stared at him. "I never saw you."

"You were sleeping. That's always been my policy, to visit while the children are asleep."

Well, that's convenient, he thought skeptically, eyeing the old fellow for signs of deception. "Why is that?" he challenged him.

"Because if people could see me right there in the room, they'd have proof that I'm real and then they wouldn't have to *believe.*

Believing is what Christmas is all about, Jake," Santa said.

Santa's answer reminded Jake of the Snow Maiden's angry words about her grandfather's stubborn refusal to prove his existence to the world. *"If they want to believe or not, that's up to them,"* she had reported him as saying.

"I would *like* people to trust in me even if they don't have any proof. Besides," Santa continued, gazing at him, "presents are nice, but they're not the main thing, are they? No. The main thing, the most important part of Christmas, Jake, is the love. And every year, when I stopped in the orphanage, I walked among all you dear, sleeping children, and I always gave you that. Like this." He held up his hand and a sprinkling of the most delicate gold dust rained down from his white-gloved fingertips.

Jake stared at it in wonder.

"Even if you can't see me or don't believe I'm there, the love soaks in—just the opposite of Spiteful Spice—and helps you find the strength to keep on going. The truth is, I can't always leave presents, even for good children. It's, just, well, it's a big world, and sometimes, I need people of goodwill like you to help me in that department. But that doesn't mean that you and the other orphans were *ever* forgotten. You always had my love."

Jake was silent for a moment, not sure what to say to that.

"Well," he forced out awkwardly, "it's nice to know at least somebody cared." Then he smiled. "I do have to admit, though, a present now and then would have been nice."

"Ah, Jake," Santa said with a smile. "The greatest Present of all was given to mankind on the very first Christmas, long ago. You think my little trinkets can ever top that?" He shook his head fondly. "No, the toys and treats I bring are only reminders of the *true* gift of His pure love, and I myself am only a shadow of who the real Giver is."

Reverently, Jake absorbed this and could only regret his preoccupation with "trinkets," as Santa had called them. Hadn't he learned on his recent trip to Wales to see the goldmine he had inherited, that material things were not the answer to all life's problems?

The old man laid a kindly hand upon his shoulder. "Now then. Are you ready to go home, Jake? I daresay Miss Helena is frantic, trying to find you and your companions."

He managed a nod. "We've got a Nativity play to put on in our country village. It means the world to Aunt Ramona."

"I know." Santa gave him a wink and said, "Follow me."

They left the office. Santa led him to the parlor in the Clauses' private living quarters within the Great Igloo.

There, Jake was reunited with his friends.

Dani came running. "Mrs. Claus said Santa has a way to get us home this very night!"

"She wouldn't tell us how, though," Isabelle chimed in.

"I'm hoping it's in the sleigh," Archie confided.

"Caw." Red looked worried that he might have to pull it. The Gryphon had come in last, shoving the parlor door closed behind him with his tail. He prowled over to sit on the floor beside Jake.

"Don't worry, Gryphon, you don't need the sleigh for this mode of travel," Santa said. "Jake, I trust you have an unused chimney somewhere in your house?"

"Yes, sir." He immediately thought of the fireplace in an extra bedchamber on the upper floor of Everton House—the one Gladwin used to come and go as she pleased.

"Excellent." Santa strolled to the fireplace on the parlor's back wall.

Jake furrowed his brow as the old man unhooked a candy cane from where it hung on a branched candelabra sitting on the mantel. To their surprise, Santa bent back the straight end of the candy cane, revealing a hidden key within.

He fitted the key into a discreet keyhole in the narrow edge of the mantel. He turned it, and they heard a click; a portion of the fireplace bricks popped forward, like the door to a hidden safe, about one foot square.

"A secret compartment?" Archie murmured.

Santa smiled at him and pushed the brick façade aside. He reached into the compartment, pulling out a sliding shelf.

On it sat a strange brass device that reminded Jake of an oversized pincushion bristling with porcelain buttons on long metal stems. Each button was painted with either a letter or a number.

"Very well," said Santa, peering over the rim of his spectacles at Jake. "Your address?"

Jake told him. The old man punched the keys, carefully spelling it out.

With that, he glanced around at them. "Righty-ho! Who wants to go first, then? One at a time, step into the fireplace."

They looked at one other in trepidation.

"Don't be alarmed, it's perfectly safe. I call this ingenious bit of sorcery my Chimneyway. You go in through here"—he gestured toward the empty fireplace—"and it spits you out on the other end at whatever address you punch in. You'll be back in London in the twinkling of an eye."

"Is it dangerous?"

"Not in the least, Miss Dani," Santa assured her, but although they trusted him, it was a strange enough mode of travel to make them all a little nervous.

"Well, I'm the eldest. I'll go first," Isabelle said, much to her brother's relief.

Gentleman that he was, Archie always felt honor-bound to protect the girls, but as a great lover of gadgets, he was keen to see the Chimneyway in action.

Isabelle stepped bravely into the fireplace, crouching down to avoid bumping her head.

"Ready?" Santa asked.

"Ready, Santa." She waved. "Goodbye!"

"Good luck," Dani said with a frown.

Then Santa hit the button labeled Go.

A loud whooshing sound of air rushed through the room like wind through a tunnel. Isabelle's hair blew around her in all directions. She looked up into the chimney with a small gasp, then suddenly disappeared in a puff of golden sparkles.

"Izzy!" Archie started forward in shock.

"Are you next? Go on, hurry!" Santa shouted over the windy clamor, and waved him on.

Archie stepped uncertainly into the fireplace. Right before their eyes, the boy genius vanished, tool-bag and all, in another poof of golden sparkles.

Jake and Dani exchanged a worried glance.

"Red?" Jake waved his pet toward the hearth.

"Becaw!" The Gryphon bounded to the fireplace and had to squash himself in before he, too, disappeared.

Whoosh!

Jake waved Dani on ahead of him as well, but instead of going directly to the Chimneyway, she ran over to Santa and gave him a hug. This done, she went dutifully to the magic fireplace, and once more—poof!

The carrot-head was gone.

Santa nodded at him with a smile. "Run along, Jake. You've still got a busy night ahead. Happy travels."

"Thanks for everything, Santa. Give my best to Mrs. C!" With the jar of Dusting Sugar tucked firmly under his arm, Jake waved farewell, then bent down and stepped into the fireplace. "Hey! I almost forgot to wish you a merry—*whoa!*"

The next thing he knew, he was tumbling out of the unused fireplace at Everton House, sprawling in a heap on the rug.

Somehow he was still holding on to the Dusting Sugar and had managed not to break the glass jar.

Jumping feet were all around him. The room was filled with the cheering of his friends, who could not contain their joy at finding themselves back safely in time for Christmas.

Teddy was also making a ruckus, barking as if to scold Dani for leaving him behind. She scooped the little brown terrier up in her arms while Red crowed in boisterous relief.

"*What* is going on up there?" a voice suddenly shouted.

Miss Helena!

The room went silent as the girls' pretty, black-haired governess marched in. "Where in the world have you been? I've been looking everywhere for you!"

Nobody said a word. Where to begin?

She looked at them in exasperation. "Fine. We'll talk about it later. For now, is everyone all right?"

"Yes, Miss Helena," they all said, nodding innocently.

She eyed them with skepticism and let out a huff, then called out the chamber door: "Never mind, Henry, I found them! They're up here!"

"Well, tell them to hurry! We're going to miss the train!" the boys' tutor hollered back from downstairs.

"He's right, you know. There's no time to lose." Miss Helena glanced at the locket watch that hung around her neck. "The train to Gryphondale leaves in half an hour. If we're not on it, we're going to miss the Nativity play—and if that happens, Her Ladyship will probably turn us all into hedgehogs. So, I suggest you hurry up!"

"Yes, ma'am."

"Sorry, miss," they said, but she had already stalked off to finish preparations for their jaunt out to the country.

"Close call," Archie murmured after she had gone.

Jake brushed the soot off his clothes. "You lot take the train with Henry and Helena. I have to go undo the bad magic from Humbug's Spiteful Spice with this stuff. Santa said it had to be done right away."

"Cutting it close, coz."

"I know, but I gave my word. Don't worry, it won't take long. I'll just shake a bit of this Dusting Sugar around those bakeries and on the gingerbread people, then I'll fly to Gryphondale on Red. Is that all right with you, boy?"

"Caw!" Red bobbed his head. He knew the way to their home village blindfolded.

Jake nodded. "Thanks."

"You'd better not be late," Dani warned. "The vicar's counting on you to be St. Joseph."

"And I, for one, don't care to try life as a hedgehog," Archie drawled.

Jake grinned at the thought. "Don't worry, I'll be there. Beard and all."

"Come *on*! Time to go! Children, honestly!" Miss Helena insisted from the direction of the entrance hall.

"Red," Jake murmured to his pet, "we'd better get out of here before Henry and Helena start asking questions."

"What are we supposed to tell them?" Dani asked.

"Just say I wanted to keep Red company on the way to Gryphondale. It's Christmas Eve. Poor fellow shouldn't have to fly out to the village all alone. It's not like we can take him on the train."

"Good enough," she replied.

"See you there," Jake said with a curt nod in farewell.

Then they parted ways.

CHAPTER NINETEEN
The Gingerbread Wars

Though it was only five thirty in the afternoon, the early darkness of winter concealed the odd sight of a boy flying on a Gryphon over London.

A light snow blew around Jake and Red as they hurtled through the sky. The night was cold, but nothing like the bitter temperatures they had experienced at the North Pole.

Meanwhile, in the streets below, shops were closing early. Clerks and masters alike were eager to go and join in the festivities with family and friends. Jake hoped Bob and Marie's bakeries were also closed by now, too.

They looked to be, he thought as Red approached.

At Jake's urging, the Gryphon landed on the flat roof of the narrow brick building that the two bakeries shared.

With the Dusting Sugar securely tucked into his coat, Jake dismounted with a word of thanks to his trusty feathered friend, then crept to the edge of the roof and peered down over the side to see if anyone was coming.

At once, he waved frantically at Red. "Get down!"

The Gryphon flattened himself as a bobby came sauntering down the street. When the helmeted constable passed on the sidewalk below them, Jake's fingers twitched with the urge to dump some Dusting Sugar on him, but he doubted it was Flanagan.

Nah, he's got all those kids. He's sure to be home with them tonight. It's Christmas Eve. Besides, if he was honest, even Jake could admit that behind that gruff exterior, Constable Flanagan was a good, stout-hearted, honest man.

After the bobby on patrol had passed below, Jake faced the

question of how to get inside. No Gladwin to let him in this time; he was going to have to use his old thieving skills.

Just as he started to get up from his crouched position, Marie herself stepped out of her shop below. Keys jangling, she turned around at the front door to lock up for the night.

Jake paused.

When he saw the haughty Frenchwoman directly underneath the spot where he knelt, he could not resist giving British Bob a bit of unseen help in the romance department. He slipped the Dusting Sugar out of his coat, flipped up the silver lid, and silently shook some out onto Mademoiselle Marie.

It swirled on the wind as it wafted down on her and mingled with the snowflakes dotting her dark velvet bonnet.

She put her keys away, none the wiser.

Merry Christmas, Bob, Jake thought with a roguish smile. *Hope it helps.*

Mademoiselle Marie walked off down the lamp-lit cobbled street, alone on Christmas Eve.

As soon as she had disappeared into the shadows, Jake stole back to Red and asked him to fly him down to the ground.

With people coming and going at odd hours, he did not want to risk being seen. The last thing he wanted was to get arrested and end up spending Christmas in the Clink. No magistrate would ever believe his story of breaking in simply to do a favor for Santa Claus.

No, his best chance at avoiding detection was to go in through the back. He could climb in through the kitchen window over the sink—he remembered it well from the night he had come here to kidnap Humbug.

In short order, Red glided him down into the alley behind the double-bakery building. Jake slid off his back and sneaked over to Chez Marie's kitchen window. He used his telekinesis to unlock it through the glass, then he lifted up the sash.

The height of the window made it rather awkward. He summoned Red over to give him a boost.

But as Jake stepped on the Gryphon's back, climbing in the window, he found himself wondering what Humbug's fate had been after his meeting with Santa.

He never did hear if the wayward elf had been sent back to his old job in Mrs. Claus's kitchen or if he had been put on reindeer stall-mucking duty, as he'd feared.

Then, squeezing through the window, Jake nearly put his foot down in a large pot full of soapy water. Apparently, it had been left to soak in the sink overnight. He fell into the kitchen with a low curse.

"Becaw?" Red pushed up onto his hind legs and peered through the window.

"I'm all right," Jake whispered in annoyance. "Stay out of sight till I come out."

As Red bobbed his head and flew away, Jake turned, hearing whispers from somewhere nearby.

"Rollio, look! Who's that coming in the window?"

"What does it matter, Juniette? Forget him. We are about to take leave of this miserable world. Oh, brokenhearted sorrow—"

"But what if he's a thief? Or a murderer?"

"So what if he is? We have resolved to die anyway."

"Yes, but not like that! What if he steps on us? Oh, Rollio, I'm frightened! His feet are so very large." She screamed. "He's seen us! He's coming this way!"

"Fear not, fair Juniette. I will protect you!" The gingerbread boy drew his tiny candy sword and brandished it as Jake warily approached. "Stay back, foul giant!"

Jake held up his hands in a token surrender. "Don't worry, I only want to speak to you." When he crouched down toward them, trying to look nonthreatening, Juniette shrieked once more and buried her pink-frosted head against her gingerbread boyfriend's shoulder. "Please, don't be afraid. Santa sent me. I'm here to help."

"Santa, you say?" Rollio asked while Juniette abruptly stopped covering her candy-button eyes. "You don't look like an elf to me."

"Nevertheless."

The gingerbread couple was standing on a low shelf above a milk pail.

Jake eyed the scene suspiciously. "Sorry if this sounds nosy, but I couldn't help overhearing. What's all this about you two killing yourselves?"

Rollio and Juniette exchanged a glance.

"We have no choice," the ginger-boy said at last. "Our families have been feuding for ages. They forbid our love. We've tried to run away together many times, but some strange curse lies on our people and always prevents us from escaping together."

"A curse?" Jake echoed.

Juniette nodded, apparently realizing he was not a threat after all. "We fall asleep when the sun rises. Then, when we awaken at nightfall, Rollio and I always find ourselves right back where we started, back at home with our families again—separated! There is no explanation."

Actually, the explanation was fairly obvious to Jake.

Mademoiselle Marie and her workers were no doubt puzzled as to why they kept finding the gingerbread pair on the floor together in the morning. They probably thought it was some kind of prank.

Jake would've bet that Marie blamed Bob for it, while Bob probably blamed Marie. Meanwhile, the shop employees simply kept putting Rollio and Juniette back where they belonged in their separate displays.

"Every night we try to elope together, but the curse is too strong. We can't go on this way!" Juniette said. "'Tis too painful."

Rollio comforted her, but directed his words at Jake. "That is why we have decided to jump into this vat of milk and drown ourselves this very night. Then we shall dissolve and be together for all eternity!"

"Welcome, oblivion!" Juniette wailed most dramatically.

"But it's Christmas Eve," Jake protested.

"No matter! We'd rather die together—end it all—than live apart!" Rollio declared.

"Oh, blimey." Jake rubbed his forehead. "Now listen here, you daft pastries. You mustn't talk like that. Nobody's killing themselves here. For your information, your relatives are at each other's throats because they have been *poisoned* with Spiteful Spice. That's what makes them fight."

"Poisoned?" they cried.

"Santa sent me with this antidote." Jake showed them the Dusting Sugar. "It's guaranteed to make them sweeter, more agreeable. I think...if I give them an extra-large dose, it might just make them end this family feud, and reconcile."

"Oh, can it really work?"

"Santa said it would, so let's go try it. In the meanwhile, you two stay away from that milk pail. Follow me."

Rollio and Juniette barely dared hope that the antidote might succeed, but at this point, they had nothing to lose. They climbed down from the supply shelf and followed at a safe distance, wary of Jake's giant feet.

He could hear their own tiny footsteps tapping along on the floor behind him as he left the kitchen and stalked out into the French pastry shop.

Moving stealthily down the dark aisle, Jake went toward the gingerbread display, taking care not to bump the *Croquembouche* Christmas tree on the end.

As he approached, he marveled to find Marie's gingerbread Versailles in an uproar.

The fanciful meringue shepherdesses beat back Bob's invading soldiers with their shepherd crooks, while their marshmallow sheep ran to and fro, bleating in distress.

The swans squawked in the blue-frosted fountain, trying to steer clear of long-haired courtiers clashing with the castle knights from downstairs.

Riders from a cookie cavalry whacked at enemy foot soldiers with their candy swizzle-stick sabers; the invaders, in turn, lobbed lemon-drop cannonballs at the walls of the gingerbread palace.

One bashed a hole in the clock tower.

Jake shook his head at the melee and took the Dusting Sugar out of his coat. Pouring a bunch of it into his hand, he stepped closer and, without warning, flung it all over them.

Not even he was sure what might happen next.

The Dusting Sugar enveloped the gingerbread Versailles for a moment in a thick cloud of fog. The angry battle sounds went quiet.

Jake heard some coughing here and there from inside the display, the confused whinny of a gingerbread warhorse.

As the sweet dust settled and (hopefully) began to work, there was a moment of stillness. Then little gingerbread soldiers started walking out of the clearing dust cloud. They wove back and forth on their frosted feet, stumbling and disoriented. One hiccupped.

Jake lifted his eyebrows.

"What happened?" one of Bob's ginger knights asked the nearest French cookie courtier, who shrugged.

"Je ne sais pas, monsieur."

Rollio was still climbing up the licorice rope that he had looped over a corner of the display table. He had let Juniette go ahead of him, so she arrived first.

The pink-haired gingerbread-girl hurried into Marie's display to check on her family. "Papa? Papa!" she called toward the palace. "Are you alive?"

Movement stirred under the rubble where two peppermint-stick columns had collapsed in the siege, bringing down the elegant white-frosted portico.

"Papa!"

"Daughter! Is that you?" came a muffled replied.

Juniette ran to help free her father from the wreckage just as Rollio reached the summit, jumping onto the display table.

"Rollio, help me!" she cried over her shoulder. "Father's trapped! I can't budge it. It's too heavy!"

"I'll get that." Jake felt a bit like his old friend, Snorri the Giant, as he reached into the display and easily lifted the roof of the broken portico off Juniette's father. "There you are."

She helped the little Sun King to his feet, but cried out in dismay to find one of his arms had cracked off.

"Oh, it's nothing, dear," he said. "A little royal icing, and I shall be good as new, I promise. I do have a question, though."

"What's that, Papa?"

"Perhaps I got knocked on the head very hard, because, for the life of me, I can't remember why we are having this war in the first place."

"Neither can I," the leader of the invading knights replied, lifting his little silver-frosted helmet as he approached.

"Father!" Rollio ran toward him.

"Son! I thought you ran away."

"I came back, Father—but there's something I must say!" He turned to all the gingerbread people and drew himself up in defiance. "Juniette and I love each other. We want to be together, no matter what!"

"B-but, son, these are our enemies!" his father spluttered. "We despise each other!"

"But why?"

Rollio's father scratched his head. He looked confused, clearly still feeling the effects of the Dusting Sugar. "We must have had a reason... Actually, now that we're all calm, these Frenchies don't really seem half bad."

"And you British do not seem like the buffoons we always

assumed."

"Maybe we could all just get along for once," Juniette said firmly.

"We could try, I suppose. The truth is, I don't really feel like fighting anymore." Rollio's father threw down his candy sword. "It does grow boring, even for a noble knight."

"I agree." The Sun King turned to his courtiers. "Lay down your arms! Well, if you still have them."

"Oh, poor Papa." Juniette picked up her father's broken arm so it would not be lost amid the rubble, then she gave him a kiss on the cheek. "Please let me marry Rollio! I love him."

"Oh, very well. If that is truly your wish, then you may have my blessing."

"Hooray!" cheered several of the gingerbread folk on both sides as Rollio and Juniette rushed together, united at last.

"Thank goodness all that's over," someone said while the little cookies applauded.

"I'm so happy, I just want to dance!" one of the courtiers shouted gleefully.

"Me too!" said a knight. "Let's have a party!"

Santa's Dusting Sugar had obviously worked, perhaps a little too well. The gingerbread people turned not just sweet and happy, but downright silly, in fact.

They started dancing around like you might expect gingerbread cookies to do if they somehow came magically to life. Even the gingerbread horses gamboled and cavorted. The fluffy marshmallow sheep came out of hiding, no longer frightened, and started bouncing to and fro. The swans squawked, the shepherdesses skipped around the fountain, and a few of the knights did back flips, which was very risky, crispy as they were.

But this was no time for a party.

For, as Jake looked on, his brow furrowed with the dawning of a dark thought, he realized he could not just leave them here.

Bizarre as it seemed, these gingerbread folk had become sentient beings, and soon, Christmas would be done.

Blast it, he had not planned on this. Indeed, time was of the essence. If he did not get a move on it, he'd be late to the Nativity.

Still, something had to be done to keep them safe. He racked his brain until the answer came.

Of course.

Looming over them, he cleared his throat to get their attention amid their celebrations. "Ahem! Excuse me—"

"*Ahhh!* Look! Giant!"

They had not even noticed him till then, but instant screams erupted.

"Run for your life!"

"No, no, it's all right, he's a friendly giant," Rollio and Juniette assured their startled kinfolk. "Even if he *is* a burglar," Juniette added under her breath.

He ignored her accusation. "My name's Jake, and Santa Claus sent me here to help you."

"Santa?" Murmurs full of wonder traveled through the crowd as the gingerbread people marveled at this news.

"I'm glad you've got the whole war business sorted out, but we've got trouble," Jake informed them. "Tomorrow's Christmas, y'see—"

"Hooray for Christmas!" they cheered.

"No! Not in your case, anyway. Think about it," he said. "Nobody needs a gingerbread display after Christmas is over. I'd give you lot till Twelfth Night, tops. Then these bakers are either going to throw you away or let their customers eat you."

A collective gasp of horror rose from the gingerbread folk.

"But don't worry," Jake said. "I'm not going to let any of that happen of you. We need to evacuate both your towns, then I'll bring you to a safe location, where you can be resettled in a new home. Just let me get a box."

"But my people down at the castle will be left behind!" Rollio's father cried.

"No worries, I'm headed there next. I'll get them, too. But we don't have much time, so everybody, please prepare to evacuate the bakery in an orderly fashion."

"Can my sheep come, too?" one of the shepherdesses asked with a pretty flutter of her lashes.

"And the horses?" a knight called.

"Squawk!"

"Of course. Swans, too. You only have to leave your buildings behind. But don't worry. Where I'm taking you, we have an excellent cook who can make you a whole new town, whatever you like. It may not be as fancy as all this, but at least you'll be safe there to, er, live out your lives."

Which was still completely odd, if you thought about it. Jake chose not to. Instead, he ran to the kitchen to fetch one of the large pasteboard cake boxes he had seen on the supply shelf.

He folded it into shape, then left it on the side of the display table so the gingerbread people could get in.

While Juniette organized the evacuation, Rollio showed Jake the secret way down into Bob's British Bakery. It turned out that his kinsmen had been using an old servant staircase as their invasion route. The gingerbread men were thinly rolled enough to be able to fit under the crack at the bottom of the drafty door.

Jake suspected that Bob and Marie used to visit each other through this stairwell during slow moments in the workday—at least, until they had ended their courtship.

Now the door to the stairwell was padlocked, but this was of little consequence to a skilled former thief.

"Better take me with you," Rollio said while Jake picked the lock with a small nail he had brought along for that very purpose, just in case. "It'll save time. My kinsmen might not trust you, but if I go, I'll let them know it's all right and that you're telling the truth."

"Good enough," Jake murmured. As soon as he had lifted the padlock off the door, he bent down and picked up the gingerbread boy, setting him on his shoulder.

Rollio braced himself, hanging on to Jake's scarf. "Ready!"

"Let's go." Jake opened the door cautiously. The stairwell was dark and a bit cobwebby, but he did not hesitate. Creeping down the stairs, he winced when one of them creaked.

Then he froze when he saw a feeble light shining in the shop below.

"Someone's still here!" Rollio whispered.

"Shh!" *Maybe someone just forgot to blow out the lantern.*

The bottom of the stairwell did not have a door, so, inching closer, Jake was able to steal a cautious glance around the corner into the lower shop.

Blast. He clenched his jaw at what he saw.

British Bob was still at work, poring over his bookkeeping ledgers on the counter by the light of a single candle. *Well, that's sad.* He looked moody, scowling down at his work, but that was no surprise.

Nobody liked being alone on Christmas Eve.

Jake, however, did not like getting arrested. Nor did he relish the thought of being attacked as an intruder by a former army officer. British Bob looked tough.

Feeling a light tap on his shoulder, Jake glanced at Rollio. The gingerbread boy pointed at the jar of Dusting Sugar.

Jake nodded.

Silently, he took it out of his coat, poured some into his hand, and then blew it into the air in Bob's direction.

It whispered down lightly onto his head and shoulders, so fine a powder that he didn't even feel it.

Jake held his breath, waiting to see what would happen.

Once more, it didn't take long to start working.

Bob let out a weary sigh that nearly snuffed his candle flame. He put his quill pen down after a moment, rubbed his eyes, then stared off into space, his ledger books forgotten.

"Oh, Marie," he said softly to himself.

With a yawn and a stretch, he rose to take a break. He unlocked his shop door and stepped out to get some fresh air.

As he gazed up at the stars, forlorn, Jake darted across the rustic-themed bakery and threw Dusting Sugar on the remaining castle knights and soldiers. They went silly, as expected—which made him wonder if the Dusting Sugar was a form of fairy dust, which could have a similar effect. Gladwin had said, after all, that Santa was technically an elf (obviously one of the large variety) and elves were related to fairies.

In any case, the Dusting Sugar made it possible for Jake to quickly collect all the castle folk on a nearby tray, which he grabbed off the counter.

"Let's go! Hurry, before he comes back!" Rollio whispered frantically. "Everyone, stay down!"

Careful to keep the tray steady, Jake sped out of Bob's shop and rushed back up the stairs without a sound.

He shut the door silently behind him.

Whew!

Heart pounding, he went back to the gingerbread Versailles and put the new arrivals in the cake box with all the others.

While they got settled, Jake took another moment to sprinkle more Dusting Sugar all around Marie's shop, in case Humbug had tainted anything else with Spiteful Spice.

After making sure he had followed all of Santa's instructions, he returned to his box of little refugees. "All right, everybody, ready to go to your new home?"

"Hurrah!" they answered.

That Dusting Sugar had certainly put them in a cheerful mood. "I'll have you there in no time," Jake said, then he closed the lid.

He whisked the box into the kitchen, but could not attempt climbing out the window while holding it. Instead, he merely unlocked the shop's back door, pulled it open, and cautiously peered out. Seeing no one, he stepped out into the alley and pulled the door shut behind him.

"Red! Where are you? Time to go!" he whispered as loudly as he dared in the direction of the roof.

Speeding around the corner to the side of the building, Jake froze at an unexpected sight in the cobbled street ahead.

Mademoiselle Marie!

Instead of walking off down the street as she had started to do when he had last seen her, something had made her turn around and come back.

Still outside as well, Bob was standing motionless in the street, staring at her.

Jake gulped, afraid he was about to get caught.

But as the seconds passed, neither baker even noticed him.

They just kept gazing at each other—first from a cautious distance, then taking a few wary steps closer.

They spoke, but Jake could not make out the words.

Whatever was said, in the next moment, he could almost hear the romantic music playing as they suddenly raced across the empty street and into each other's arms. They embraced with the snow sprinkling down on them all the while.

Awww, thought Jake with a cheeky grin.

But when the sprig of mistletoe hanging from the wrought-iron lamppost above them required the reconciling couple to kiss, he looked away in embarrassment.

Thankfully, Red pounced onto the snowy ground beside him at that moment.

"Finally!" Jake slung a leg over his back. "We'd better get going," he said in a low tone. "We need to make a stop at Beacon House."

Red swiveled his head around and looked curiously at the box. "Becaw?" he asked, as if to say, *You stole a cake?*

"No, it's the gingerbread people. We need to drop them off before we head out to Gryphondale, savvy?"

"Caw!"

Jake held onto the cake box tightly as Red gathered speed, running up the side street.

Wings pumping, he launched into the air and flew right over Bob and Marie, but still kissing under the mistletoe, they never even noticed.

CHAPTER TWENTY
The Christmas Wish

Santa himself had called Jake brave, but even he found it slightly terrifying to be holding on to the Gryphon with one hand as they soared high above the rooftops of London; his other arm, of course, was busy clutching the box full of gingerbread people.

He was scared to death of dropping it. Dozens of lives were at stake, after all.

"Uh, Red, could you fly a little lower, please?" he asked nervously.

His winged friend obliged him, but Jake didn't really relax until the beast touched down once more on the roof of Beacon House.

The great lantern with its yew tree silhouette was shining in the rooftop cupola—a secret sign to those in the know, that the old Tudor mansion on the Thames was a safe haven for magical beings.

Well, this situation certainly qualified, Jake thought.

Beacon House had plenty of unused bedchambers. He would set the gingerbread people up in one of the extra rooms, then hurry on to Gryphondale to play his part in the Nativity (no matter how stupid he knew he was going to feel).

Ignoring a frisson of stage fright, he continued telling his little passengers about Mrs. Appleton as he slid off Red's back, still carefully holding the box steady. "She has house brownie blood, you know, which means she's an excellent baker. I'm sure she can make you whatever sort of new gingerbread village you might like."

"Can she fix Papa's arm?" Juniette asked.

"Oh, I'm sure of it. I'll bet she can even paint you with some sort of shellac or varnish, so you don't ever crack or get stale."

"Oh, that would be wonderful!"

They were very excited.

"Be right back, Red." The Gryphon remained behind on the roof while Jake went in through the little rooftop door on the side of the cupola. Then he carried his passengers down the spiral stairs, and a moment later, stepped out into the upper hallway, as before.

He opened a few of the empty bedchamber doors along the corridor to find the gingerbread folk a nice room where they'd be comfortable.

"This one looks good." It had a large canopy bed, a writing desk, a fireplace, and two tall windows.

Jake started to set them down.

"Oh, not on the floor, please! There could be mice," the little Sun King warned.

"Ah. Of course." He went and set their box down on the middle of the bed instead. It was soft and would give them plenty of room to spread out.

Seeing that this pleased them, Jake folded down one side of the cake box to let them out. Then he went and lit the oil-lantern on the desk to give them some light.

As the lamp illuminated the chamber, he spotted a pad of paper and a few pencils on the desk. He brought them over to the bed. "Here. You can use these to start sketching your ideas for your new town."

"Oooh, and plan our perfect wedding!" Juniette exclaimed, fluttering her lashes at Rollio.

"Er, whatever," Jake mumbled. "I'll go let Mrs. Appleton know you're here. Afraid I can't stay, but I'll come back and visit you in a few days, and bring my friends to meet you."

He could not wait to see Dani and Archie and Isabelle's faces when they met the living gingerbread folk.

"Thank you so much for everything!" they cried.

"You're very welcome. Happy Christmas—and no fighting," he said with a smile.

"Goodbye, Jake! Goodbye, giant boy!" they called, waving and hopping around on the mattress.

He gave them a final nod of farewell, then stepped out into the hallway and pulled the door shut. *Better hurry.* It was no short ride out to Gryphondale and he had not planned on having to make this stop.

Determined to get out of there as quickly as possible, he jogged the rest of the way down the formal hallway, past its row of old paintings whose eyes always seemed to follow you.

At the end of the hallway, he came to the top of the ornate staircase that overlooked the foyer.

"Mrs. Appleton?" he called.

No response.

He frowned and started down the stairs. "Mrs. Appleton?"

Not here? Drat. What about the butler?

"Mr. Mayweather? Anybody home?"

The minute Jake stepped down into the foyer, his gaze slammed to a halt on the Christmas tree in the corner—with the pile of presents beneath it.

The presents he and his friends had bought for the orphans.

Still waiting to be delivered, for it was Christmas Eve.

Oh, no...

Jake paled as he realized his oversight. "Oh, no, no, no," he whispered to himself, raising a hand to his forehead. *"Idiot!"*

In all the excitement of returning Humbug to the North Pole, Jake had completely forgotten about the presents they had gathered for the orphanage.

Now what?

Their plan had been to deliver the presents and somehow make it look like Santa had done it. But now Jake faced a painful choice. *Whom do I disappoint? Aunt Ramona or the orphans?*

He could either hightail it to Gryphondale to be in the Nativity play or take the presents to the orphanage. After all the hours they had lost on their adventure, there was no longer enough time to do both.

Blast it. Jake crossed the foyer to check the library in the vague hope that either the housekeeper or the butler was actually at home. Maybe, done with their duties for the day, they were relaxing and had just dozed off by the fire.

He knew that either of the kindly old souls would have been happy to deliver the presents for him.

But no.

The library where he had interrogated Humbug held no Mrs. Appleton, no Mr. Mayweather, and no cozy fire in the hearth, as he'd hoped. He walked in, glanced around, and sighed.

The butler and housekeeper must have gone out to enjoy the Christmas Eve festivities, along with the rest of the world.

Well, if it came down to it, he knew what he would choose.

Santa *had* said he needed people to help him once in a while, and surely Aunt Ramona would understand. He could be in the village Nativity next year, he thought, never mind that his not showing up would make a very bad impression on the whole village full of neighbors who were only just getting to know him.

One last possibility occurred to him.

Maybe they're in the kitchen! he thought, hoping against hope.

But as he turned and headed for the door, he suddenly heard a strange rustle in the fireplace behind him.

He spun around just in time to see a flurry of silver snowflakes rushing out of the hearth, accompanied by a smattering of red-and-green sparkles.

Jake's jaw dropped as the Snow Maiden stepped out of the fireplace as coolly as you please, with Humbug by her side.

He was amazed to see her, especially since she looked so...different.

Instead of wearing bizarre high-fashion clothes and trying to look older, she was dressed in a fairly normal-looking blue coat with a hood and sleeves trimmed in white fur.

Her blond hair hung over her shoulders in two braids, with a sprig of holly tucked behind her ear.

From her rosy cheeks to the smile presently on her face instead of her former bored scowl, *now* she fit the description of the Snow Maiden of Eastern Europe's Christmas legends.

"Hello, Jake," she said ever so casually, sauntering into the library.

"What are you doing here?" he burst out when he finally found his voice. "And Humbug?"

The erstwhile grumpy elf grinned at him.

"Grandmother sent me," the Snow Maiden said. At his blank look, she added, "To deliver those presents for you?"

"Along with some real holiday magic!" Humbug chimed in.

Jake laughed aloud. "Mrs. Claus, I love you."

"I think she knows," the Snow Maiden drawled.

"Beg your pardon, but this is quite a surprise. I thought you hated Christmas."

"Well..." She dropped her gaze. "Once Christmas Eve arrived, I started thinking about my former duties, helping Grandpapa bring the toys, and I... Well, in the end, I didn't want to be left out," she said with a slight pout. "Besides, I owe you, I suppose, for keeping you and your friends prisoner. Let's just say this is my own little way of making up for it."

Jake shook his head, amazed. "Apology accepted."

"So where are these presents, then?"

"Right in here." He led them into the foyer. "I'll write down the address of the orphanage for you—"

"Please," she cut him off with a superior glance. "I *am* Santa Claus's granddaughter, Jake. Give me a little more credit than that."

He laughed in surprise. "Sorry." He really could hardly believe his good fortune at her arrival. "You're sure you don't mind?"

"Not at all. Hopefully, this should help me get back into Grandfather's good graces. Humbug, put the presents in the sack."

"Yes, ma'am!"

"Ha, and you were worried you'd be put on reindeer stall-mucking duty," Jake said to the elf, who was whisking all the gifts into the wide-mouthed sack they had brought along.

"Oh, I was!" Humbug answered. "But then Mrs. Claus told me to go help Snow Maiden with this mission. Believe me, I was glad to tag along."

"Good, then you can carry the sack, Humbug," Snow Maiden said. "Happy Christmas, Jake." Her blue eyes sparkled as she sauntered back to the fireplace in the library. The little elf struggled along after her under the giant sack filled with toys.

Jake followed them, still mystified. "I really do appreciate this."

"I know," she answered lightly, stepping into the fireplace. "Don't worry, we'll give them a good show. Won't we, Humbug?"

"Yes, ma'am!"

"Ta-ta." The Snow Maiden tapped the side of her nose just like Santa had done; Humbug held onto the fur-lined hem of her coat as she went shooting up the chimney.

In the blink of an eye, she was gone—as if she was never there, but for the eddy of sparkling snowflakes she had left behind.

"Huh," Jake whispered at length, a smile spreading across his face.

Now it was time to get on with his own Christmas.

As the grandfather clock in the foyer started bonging the hour, he dashed a quick note to Mrs. Appleton about the gingerbread people, then raced upstairs, and back out onto the roof, rejoining Red.

"To Gryphondale, boy!"

There was no time to lose.

* * *

Red flew hard for nearly two hours.

When they finally approached their quaint home village in the English countryside, Jake saw the crowd was already gathering in the tiny town square around a cheerful bonfire. The people were mulling about, drinking wassail, laughing with their neighbors, and watching entertainers juggle fiery torches.

As soon as Red touched down on the elegant back terrace of Griffon Castle, Jake was already taking off his coat as he ran to get into his St. Joseph getup.

Just a stone's throw across the meadows, over at Bradford Park, Archie and Isabelle and Dani were also donning their Christmas pageant costumes.

It was a bit of a scramble at the end there, but the next thing Jake knew, he was standing by the manger in the middle of the Nativity play.

He felt the strangest jumble of emotions, like the warm glow of the candles that all the village children were holding had got inside his chest.

Maybe some of Santa's magic Dusting Sugar had absorbed into his skin, because he didn't complain once about the fake beard, silly as it looked; he got there on time; and he smiled from ear to ear as the whole community gathered to honor the miracle of the Savior's birth and sing the old hymns.

He wasn't the only one overcome by the love, either. To *everybody's* shock, even the stern, proud Dowager Baroness Bradford (their Great-Great Aunt Ramona) wiped a brief tear from her eye.

That was when he knew that Santa was right. When it came to Christmas, the only thing that really mattered was the love.

There was, however, a great mystery that year at the annual Nativity play.

The villagers could not figure out how the vicar, in charge of the production, had managed to make the Christmas star fly up onto the top of the stable all by itself.

"Oooo, ahhhh," the people watching said.

They later concluded that it must have been one of young Master Archie's ingenious inventions, some sort of newfangled sparklers, or what's-it, pyrotechnics.

But from his Joseph vantage point beside the manger, Jake knew the truth. He spotted the telltale golden sparkle-trail, and grinned behind his awful fake beard.

Little did the villagers suspect that they had a real live royal garden fairy in their midst. Up flew Gladwin in a star costume, using fairy magic to shine with all her might.

* * *

It was not until a few days after Christmas that Jake returned to London and was finally able to go and visit the orphanage that had once been his home.

He was dying to see what his old friends thought of "Santa" finally bringing them presents. Nevertheless, it was difficult for him to face that dreary place again, with all its painful memories.

Life was better now, he reminded himself.

Besides, he had to find out if Santa had upheld his end of the bargain and fulfilled Jake's hard-won Christmas wish.

It didn't take long to get his answer.

He braced himself as he went in, but after visiting with his fellow orphans for a while, he looked around the stark, chilly dormitory and had to ask: "It's good to see you all again, but where's Petey?"

"Oh, Jake, it's the most wonderful thing!" one of the ragged girls said breathlessly. "Just this morning, he got adopted by the nicest family!"

As she went on to describe them, Jake listened rapturously to the details, but he was so happy they barely sank in.

He couldn't believe it. Santa had come through.

He had got his Christmas wish.

EPILOGUE
Crumbs of a Mystery

Nobody ever *could* explain where all the gingerbread people had disappeared to on that Christmas Eve.

It became one of the great mysteries of the London baking and confectionary world.

It even made the papers, and hatched fanciful stories of gingerbread people coming to life and fleeing the shops on their own. Oh, but everyone said that was silly. Only children believed such things.

The adults took a more worldly view of the matter.

Bob and Marie had always suspected each other of this petty vandalism, but once they were reconciled, they both realized neither had been tampering with the other's gingerbread displays, as they had assumed.

Very strange.

The best they could figure was that a family of mice with a particular taste for gingerbread must have got in somehow, and eaten all the poor gingerbread folk.

Still, as delicious as everything was in their shops, it seemed odd that none of the other baked goods had been touched.

And so, the mystery remained.

Not even the stalwart bobby, Constable Flanagan, could solve it...

But he had his suspicions.

THE END

Dear Reader,

We'd like to wish you and yours a Merry Christmas and a joyous holiday season. Thank you for picking up **Jake & The Gingerbread Wars**. We hope it brought a smile to your face. Writing this holiday adventure was a lot of fun for the two of us, especially coming up with all the chapter title puns. We very much enjoy letting our imaginations run wild in the fantasy Victorian setting and spending time with Jake and the gang and all the magical creatures. But we wanted to mention something...

Since this Christmas tale is a standalone story, we realized that this might be your first visit to the world of The Gryphon Chronicles. If you'd like to read more of this epic seven-book series, we recommend you start with **Book One, The Lost Heir**. In this story, Jake is introduced for the first time, along with his friends—and some key enemies! You'll get to see how he was lost from his parents as a baby and how his relatives finally found him again.

This fun, wholesome middle grade series is recommended for ages 10 and up, (grownups welcome!) but younger kids who are avid readers should do fine with these books, too. And it's worth mentioning, the Christmas tale you just read is the lightest of the stories, and also, the full novels are two to three times the length of **Jake & The Gingerbread Wars**—a big series for you and your family to really sink your teeth into.

Thank you so much for spending your leisure time with us! Wishing you all good things for the new year.

Best wishes,
E.G. Foley

The Complete Gryphon Chronicles Series:

ABOUT THE AUTHORS

E.G. FOLEY is the pen name for a husband-and-wife writing team who live in Pennsylvania. They've been finishing each other's sentences since they were teens, so it was only a matter of time till they were writing together, too.

Like his kid readers, "E" (Eric) can't sit still for too long! A bit of a renaissance man, he's picked up hobbies from kenpo to carpentry to classical guitar over the years, and holds multiple degrees in math, science, and education. He treated patients as a chiropractor for nearly a decade, then switched careers to venture into the wild-and-woolly world of teaching middle school, where he was often voted favorite teacher. His students helped inspire him to start dreaming up great stories for kids, until he recently switched gears again and left teaching to become a full-time writer and author entrepreneur.

By contrast, "G" (Gael, aka Gaelen Foley) has had *one* dream all her life and has pursued it with maniacal intensity since the age of seventeen: writing fiction! After earning her Lit degree at SUNY Fredonia, she waited tables at night for nearly six years as a "starving artist" to keep her days free for honing her craft, until she finally got The Call in 1997. Today, with millions of her twenty-plus romances from Ballantine and HarperCollins sold in many languages worldwide, she's been hitting bestseller lists regularly since 2001. Although she loves all her readers, young and old, she admits there's just something magical about writing for children.

You can find the Foleys on Facebook/EGFoleyAuthor or visit their website at www.EGFoley.com. They are hard at work on their next book.

Thanks for Reading!

81028797R00102

Made in the USA
Columbia, SC
15 November 2017